Vade Mecum

by

Tito Perdue

Books by Tito Perdue

Lee (1991)
The New Austerities (1994)
Opportunities in Alabama Agriculture (1994)
The Sweet-Scented Manuscript (2004)
Fields of Asphodel (2007)
The Node (2011)
Morning Crafts (2013)
Reuben (2014)
The Builder: William's House I (2016)
The Churl: William's House II (2016)
The Engineer: William's House III (2016)
The Bachelor: William's House IV (2016)
Cynosura (2017)
Philip (2017)
Though We Be Dead, Yet Our Day Will Come (2018)
The Bent Pyramid (2018)
The Philatelist (2018)
The Smut Book (2018)
The Gizmo (2019)
Love Song of the Australopiths (2020)
Materials for All Future Historians (2020)
Journey to a Location (2021)

Vade Mecum

by

Tito Perdue

Standard American Publishing Company-
Brent, Alabama
2021

CONTENTS

One

I don't really have anything to say to those persons who house their books in *metal* shelving. From the earliest times, I understood that artifacts so essential comport solely with shelves of maple or cherrywood, or occasionally pine if the grain be remarkable and the lacquer mellow enough. Considered as a function of the wallpaper, pinewood does sometimes deliver a pleasing contrast to the much darker leather-bound volumes that form a major proportion of the collection under consideration here. Fourteen inches in depth, wooden shelving can sustain as many as 34–37 octavo titles over a span of thirty-five inches or less. Now, I define such a shelf as of at least ¾ inch in thickness.

I need hardly add that in order to ward away the mildew and dust, each range be protected by a facing panel of glass clear enough to let the books be seen in all the appealing imperfections they actually possess. I can pull up a chair and open any of these books I wish.

This, then, was the disposition of things in December when Lathrop entered without knocking and went for a glass of cider. I hardly drink anything these days apart from spirits and red rosé. He said:

"No, I was sure I'd find you here, reading in this dim light."

"I'm not so sure," said I, "that I'd say that I was actually *reading* just now.

"Just checking something?"

"Yes, that's more accurate."

"Verifying something. Something in that large book."

"Yes."

Viewed through the bottom of his wine glass, his nose was bigger than a pickle, the pores large enough to shelter ticks. Steeped in an especially aggressive form of neo-Confucianism, I always kept a safe distance between us.

"And I don't think those books are as almighty precious as you say either."

"What did you say?"

"Precious."

He sauntered off, taking with him the glass that I would have to retrieve later on. Further down the hall, I espied a bar of dull yellow light in the hiatus beneath Milbrook's door. A good reader but poor sleeper, he would have tried to drug himself with the half-dozen pharmaceuticals arrayed on the adjoining pillow. He possessed the best bed in the building, the carved headboard reaching nearly to the ceiling.

I continued with my work, a perpetual effort to reorganize my collection by color, height, and provenance, qualities that conflicted with each other in most cases out of ten. But in truth, I had pretty much given up the project and instead of that, I was reading a seventeenth-century account of doings in Cornwall near the end of that century. I doubt there be more than a hundred of us who still acknowledge those events, never mind the aftereffects that must have made of life a living hell-on-earth for the survivors. However, these, too, are dead by now, and their descendants neither acknowledge nor care about it any longer. And in short, these are the sort of distressing truths that finally turned me away from life and into this out-of-the-way building where I now stand, as it were, interrogating myself and you.

Two

This night was not of course greatly unlike others of the same kind, save insofar as I was to meet with an untoward thing that came upon me at just after midnight. I had been wandering and thinking, sometimes probing into the bars and shops still conducting business at that late hour. I had been looking into jewelry-store windows at all those bracelets and rings, some of them possessed of a quality about halfway between great music and modern advertising design. Though they are not the costliest of gems, I had a particular sympathy for milk-white Australian *opals* wherein a person may sometimes perceive traces of other elements and other minerals that tend to crowd these naturally-occurring stones. Getting down on my knees and into my glasses, I focused upon an oblong affair of about the size of an acorn teeming with blue and yellow streaks not unlike lightning sticks. Viewed from different points of view, the views proved different, too. I saw then a tiny irregularity of about the size of a molecule that looked like a tiny brown bear prowling the lower precincts of the jewel. And yet, not all the opals the world over could equal the peculiarity of that emulsifying down-and-out five-story building that lodges *me*.

I was about to arise and continue on when I was disrupted by a blue-clad constable who lifted me from my somewhat embarrassing position. I was tempted to reveal my membership in our little coalition of crime-fighters, old men mostly, who have banded together on the fourth floor. My identification card was laminated and offered my photo, fingerprints, and genome, but I didn't wish to pull rank on this good-intentioned official.

"Ha!" said I, much embarrassed. "No, I was just trying to get a better look at some of these opals."

"Sure, you were." He came nearer, inspecting the display window as if I might have been trying to get it open. Finding nothing of that sort, he re-holstered his weapon and also began to appraise the merchandise. He was attracted to emeralds, no question about that, but when at last he spoke, it was on another subject altogether.

"I wouldn't give you a nickel for all the goddamn little white opals in Argentina."

"I see!"

"*Black* opals, that's the real shit."

"I see. And do you have any little black opals yourself?"

He stepped back. "Why do you ask?"

"They tend to get all fuddled up with pyrites, is what I understand."

"Wouldn't give you a nickel for all the pie rights . . . Hey, where you going all of a sudden!"

I took two steps more. His face was as undifferentiated as a pancake's, nor was the rest of him a great deal better.

"Thought I'd head on back," said I. "To my lodging."

"My wife—she used to be my wife—had a couple of black ones. But she died."

"So, who has them now?"

"My sister took 'em. She's already got three of her own."

"Gosh. Altogether, they must be worth quite a lot by now."

"You kidding? The boy needs to be in jail."

He was urging me forward more speedily than I like to go. It was also chillier than I like to see, and a fair number of the streetlamps had expired. A good half-mile from my home in the slums, we had intruded into a neighborhood appreciably worse than my own. Laundry had been set out to dry from some of the upper stories and a fat man—he did not wave back—was sitting on the sill of a fifth-floor window.

"You sure do walk fast," I flattered the agent.

"No, I'm just average. It's you what's got the problem."

I thanked him and then soon after turned eastwardly, steering myself by rote toward a bent building made of cardboard or, possibly, corrugated tin, as it seemed to me. It housed, this structure, an enterprise of poor reputation well-known from newspaper accounts, as also from the blonde presenter on television channel WOOT. Admired for her pert nose and décolletage, she often reported about happenings at the "Retort," a twenty-story address the New York police seldom cared to enter. Formed not of tin but of something else, the structure begins to bend at about the eighth floor, acuminating in a sloped roof forested with antennae of all sorts pointing off in the usual directions.

I made a detour and then trudged counter-clockwise to approach the somewhat sullied river that represents the received boundary of the island on this side. The traffic was bad, and a luminescent drone had come to a stop about thirty feet overhead. A man and his dog, or someone's, were sleeping athwart the sidewalk where a great many bright red ants were feeding around a pool of spilt whiskey or mayhap urine, scenes that have become much more often witnessed since the penultimate president, a weak executive under control of the northeastern mandarinate. Let me add that I am constantly aware of those more advanced creatures in the cosmos who can monitor my mind. Suddenly, sniffing my presence, the dog jumped back and gave voice, awakening the man and prompting me forward at the same time.

I passed a late-night saloon full of human sewage, the "music" pouring from the yawing door some of the most awful the western world has thus far produced. Tired, chilled, old, intoxicated on cigarettes, I wished me home again.

Three

Arriving back at said home again, I saluted the three old men loitering about the pool table and then proceeded straightway to my three-room billet with its book collection, its microwave oven, telescope, and other cultural paraphernalia. But prior to divesting myself of my galoshes and heavy jacket, I went immediately to the window to verify that I had been followed. This window, too narrow to admit a human person, supplied an excellent view of the street, or most of it anyway, not to mention the opposite sidewalk with its twenty-four-hour human traffic. Removing with care the contents of my pockets, I organized the material in order of size on my writing desk. Heedless of small coinage, I simply stacked the quarters and dimes into unreliable piles and positioned them to one side. The main thing was my wallet, currently holding some four thousand dollars in large bills and a lesser amount in smaller denominations. I had a cigarette lighter, the coins already mentioned, and half a dozen barbed .357 magnum cartridges weighing between one and one and one-half ounces each. Perhaps you haven't seen what those babies can actually do. The revolver itself was conveyed, not in my pocket, but rather a blue suede ankle holster which I now also removed and lay on the table.

I have once before alluded to the mission that has brought us together, us old man with all our garrulities and bad procedures. Widowers all, our children have grown up and gone away while *their* children are not the sort with whom we can comfortably communicate. We were inclined therefore to keep away from them.

Returning to my narrow window, I lifted my binoculars and focused on an old woman driving a car. The uptown buildings were spangled with bright blue and green lights revealing where nighttime office thralls—I used to be like that myself—were working into the wee hours. Photographing this scene with my mind, I could not but wonder how the future would appraise this era, and whether cities would grow ever larger or return at last to pasture. You can assume my preference.

Yesterday, I was saying that our city government had fallen into mostly female hands and no longer had the testicles to grant *real* punishment to the ten hundred thousand malefactors creating a hell-on-earth for the town's remaining white population. White ourselves and approaching death, we had decided it were time to . . . do things.

We were all of us old men, most of us, saving only *Sophie* who by agreement was allowed to stay with Dwayne. A decent-looking woman of about 5'4", she supplied the only bit of cheer and optimism that had so far found a way into the building. Too, she sometimes baked cookies for the pensioners, which is to say until about two-and-a-half months had gone by, and her disposition began to spoil, and the cookies came less and less often to those waiting for them. It wasn't easy to be a woman in that crowd of bad-natured men, some of us still libidinous in spite of the years. And then, too, we were conspicuously ugly, disfigured by age, and loath to uncover our faces.

The things that men do, are they important? People of our sort—silent, humped, and full of knowledge—have not the slightest influence on public affairs, nor would the world have allowed it. Pushed off into dark corners, only by the most indirect means are we sometimes able to forestall change and offer small hindrances to the young. Reduced to using our money, of which we possess rather more than the common ruck, we are still able to write to newspapers, proffer condemnations, absorb some portion of public funding, preempt hospital beds, and tantalize our progeny with our un-declared estates.

We gather most times in Taw's half-room apart-ment. He would have a quantity of forty-proof wine for us as also a bowl of cashews and crackers with paste. Entering one-by-one, we would salute the fellow and hasten to our places. It would be dark by this time, and the downtown searchlights would have already been scanning the windows of Taw's ninth-floor apartment setting. Milbrook's dog was there, an ochre-colored creature who ten days earlier had fallen into a sudden-onset fugue state leaving him with a permanent squint. Highly cerebral for a dog, yet he had not the least idea of what he looked like.

Tonight, the topic was all sorts of things, the start-ing point for the cultural revolution we envisioned for our lapsed century. Blephy spoke first. A handsome figure of a man by previous standards, he had lost his hair to cancer while his massy goiter, decorated with tattoos, made it impossible for him to wear a tie. A re-spected psephologist with degrees from a quantity of places, he had devised a suffrage system that finally gave weight, not to the *number* of votes, but their qual-ity. Ten votes each for military heroes, twenty for opera singers, etc. Once adopted, the reform would have simplified national elections and returned to white males their earned advantages. Not an especially robust man, he had just three days earlier citizen-arrested without assistance a 260-pound jigaboo yielding a switchblade knife.

Followed then a short discussion on the nation's food supplies. Grain production had been good this year in Iowa and only slightly worse in Kansas. The price of butter by contrast had continued its untoward rise. We then abbreviated the meeting by a show of hands and finished off the cider. One of the fellows had put on a disreputable film, but I was keen to get back to my station and into the next chapter of Sima Qian's *Records of the Grand Historian,* to my mind the most entrancing of all long-form histories, not excluding those of Theopompus or al Tabari.

My bedstead is encompassed with a number of things. Apart from digital devices, beverages, pharmaceuticals, and Glocks, I maintain a select bedside library of some dozen sixteenth- and seventeenth-century gold-tooled volumes acquired or borrowed by me over a long lifetime of unrelenting reading. Equipped thus, I could sustain a month-long siege by inside and outside forces intent upon my harm. In addition to that, Milbrook's dog is sometimes allowed to stay with me.

Now this Milbrook is an ambiguous personality who tends to run in several directions at once. He has never disagreed with anyone, insofar as I've been able to find. Further, he is a solid-looking organism who remains in one place for long periods, facilitating his achievement as a Grand Master in international chess competition. Able to bench-press 80% of his own 217 pounds, I sought never to irritate this person ever. On the contrary! He has weapons, too, and often we will do target practice (with silencers) in the hall itself. Pedestrians down in the street below—and there are always many of these—haven't the least suspicion of the risks they run from people like us.

Eighty-one years old but still making efforts at happiness, he had not long ago auto gendered back to male again and with the aid of chemicals had turned himself into a more or less normal-seeming human being, or "on the surface" at any rate. Given that granite-like surface construed with the help of transplants, his was an intimidating presence both in the dormitory as in the street down below. I have seen New Yorkers of the or-

dinary kind scatter from his path, which is to say during those brief interludes when he actually participates
in the movement of crowds, something he seldom does
save when occasions of that kind enter the sphere of
his activity. And in short, he was a treasured member of
our fourth-floor organization.

It is not perhaps too early now to expose the purpose of our group; instead, I propose at this juncture to
describe how we came to occupy this besought site offering views of some of the most startling parts of the
city. In brief, our primary assignment was to rectify the
condition of our country and set it aright, a long-term
project necessitating a certain quantity—we do not yet
know the total—of arranged deaths. Meanwhile, for us
to take up residence in this place, our benefactor had
been required to force two bills through the up-state
legislature mandating living space at low cost for essential personnel of our special type. A peculiar man admittedly, he had lost two sons in the country's humani-
tarian efforts in the Near and Middle East and sought
revenge by dedicating to us his fortune, some four and
a half hundred million earned through the importation
of cocoa beans from Honduras. Not destined ever to
meet the man, we had to respect the privacy provided
him by his grandson at an institution in the Adiron-
dacks.

Adjusting my lamp, I opened to page 31 of Simon
Daines' *Orthoepia Anglicana* (1640), an oilcloth-bound
and somewhat irresponsible treatise in poor physical
repair. I had refueled my lantern just two days ago, but
already the instrument was sputtering, leaving the corners of my room in full darkness. There might be individuals lurking in each of those areas for all I knew.
Aware of that, I used the occasion to take one of my
medicines, a popular psychotropic costing seventeen
dollars per capsule. It's difficult for a person of my sort

to be calm amid this century's perturbations while at the same time abiding in a residence as unpredictable as this one. Suddenly, just that moment, I was disturbed by a bright luminescence penetrating my thick curtains and then just as quickly draining away again. I leapt to window and brought my telescope into focus. Was I the only one to have seen it? The city itself was sleeping soundly by now, apart from some score of pedestrians down below who had come to a halt and were pointing imprecisely at an explosion that had transpired a million years ago at a distance of God knows how many light years. I knew of course that at light speed, a million years ago translates precisely to an equal number of light-years distance.

Numbers like these terrify ordinary people.

I read two pages more at good speed and then another half-page with deteriorating interest. The illustrations were quite good, however, one of them startlingly redolent of Milbrook's visage. Meanwhile, someone was tapping gingerly at my chamber door, no doubt one of the fifth-floor cases in search of money, or alcohol, or conversation. I ignored it. By this time, I calculated, the light from that supernova would have escaped the galaxy altogether and might by now be well along on its voyage to other destinations in the time-space continuum, very far away.

Four

As I was starting to say, the man who brought us together in our tattered hotel cannot by agreement be given a name. An active policeman, or detective rather, who had earned obligations from certain members of the City Council, it was he who initially procured funding from an unrevealed man of wealth and to whom we reported on a more or less random basis as events required. Fifty years old, or slightly older, he had lost his daughter to a black jigaboo rapist who had had the grace to slice off her breasts and carry them away. A white person can imagine the effect upon his psyche, already made pessimistic by his years in the fifth precinct. Following his wife's suicide (by rope), he abandoned himself to drugs and television and passed eighteen months under psychiatric care.

He turned hard and cold. Anyone entering his residence would have found guns of various types all over the place. Though allowed to inspect the daily ingress of newly arrested negroes, he had no means to identify the one, or ones, he sought. "Kill 'em all!" he opined. But this was not allowed by the supervisor on duty at the time.

Two years of this and he did try to form a companionable connection with a downtown waitress, an attractive, somewhat attractive, divorcée with children. He realized of course that her attentions would forever be more for them than for him, a traditional course of action for that gender. Even so, he continued to patronize that restaurant and leave large tips.

Came April the following year, he rejoined the detective squad and served some three-quarters of a year before quitting the profession altogether and consecrating himself thereafter to our small group of large men and Sophie. Bringing us together, he told what was expected in return for free rent and half a dozen get-out-of-jail coupons:

"Identify them by their trousers and haircuts, but do not, repeat do *not* try to arrest them. I have friends for that."

The following day, a Tuesday as I recall, was expected to be better and was. I leapt from bed to the sound of dogs calling from the hills. There are of course no such sounds in big cities, nor that of crickets or tree frogs either. I *was* able to hear a screaming ambulance running at full tilt down Forrest Lane. I dressed, bathed, micturated, passed a razor over my beard, and applied shaving cream to the area. According to the mirror, I had nicked an artery, a small one, just to the left side of my considerable nose. I had cumulated almost no sleep during the foregoing black night and in total had read not more than seven pages in Taw's copy of the *Oneirocritica* of Artemidorus. Accordingly, my soul and head were foggy for want of sleep and my gait more risible than ordinarily.

I crossed the street, putting myself in danger of two enormous trucks that seemed to be coinciding upon me purposefully. I drew my Glock—at my age, I have less to lose than anyone—but never used it. I was smoking, smoking in open view, yea, and thinking thoughts that were *far* out of view.

I whistled as I moved. My accustomed restaurant was full of mid-day business types wherefore I continued on to a less expensive rendezvous called *Good Eats* situated some thousand rods to the northeast. A person of my sort can relax in a place like this, provided he sit with his back to the wall. One prostitute, one only, sat across from me, a good-looking presentation full of all sorts of nerve endings. She would not be interested in me, however, not for all the renminbi in China. Her hosiery was dark, but no one had told her that her skirt was much too short.

I asked the waitress for waffles and sausage and watched as she trundled back to the kitchen. Weighing hardly five stone, I divined that she had experienced two divorces thus far and three worthless sons mulcting her for drug money. Why had she elected to go on living?

Love, we must suppose.

The music here was especially poor, though I've sometimes heard even worse from the fifth floor. But the coffee was good and the sausage straight off the bone. I have an abiding need for sweets, and for that reason I had formed a half-inch pool of black maple syrup and set my waffle adrift on it. No one I had ever known had the least suspicion of where I was at that point in time. And anyway, most of them are dead by now.

I can't complain. Grateful for the government's compassion (not to mention our patron's bequest), I am given food stamps, possess more than three-quarters of a million in 6% debentures, 520 platinum coins, 4,300 biotechnology shares, and have paid no taxes in nine years. My fingerprints have been reconfigured, and with the help of a former friend—all my friends are former friends—my birth certificate, driver's license, passport, voter's I.D., library card, genome and other identifications have all been amended. Indeed, nothing remains of me apart from two offspring of opposite races residing purportedly in Europe and Asia.

But now, the moment had come to report to the Brooklyn Health Clinic, a necessary visit if I hoped to continue my disability checks. Though I've never actually used it for its designated purpose, my cane has a lead-filled knob of a size about halfway between a large and small orange. Today, I was transporting less than a thousand dollars, most of it contained in a flat silver flask used by some for whisky. Positioned in front of my heart, this inconspicuous utility also functions as a safeguard against bullets. I also carried perhaps an eighth-pound of silver coinage in my left pocket and six rounds of .357 ammunition in my right. I carried a nail-clipper, a vial of serotonin, two subway tokens, and an expired opera ticket to a performance of *Norma*. I carried other things, too, but apart from the typical lint, can't remember what they were.

Equipped thus, I hobbled past a spate of brokerages, internet cafes, and snot-nose coffee shops. The people I encountered had faces that would have astounded previous Americans. Crossing to Sunflower Street, I followed an overweight negress in and out of an imported merchandise outlet where for a moment she seemed ready to purloin an expensive-looking handbag with a leathern drawstring. I photographed her behind quarters with my ingenious telephone but then soon after deleted the picture after admitting that she had done nothing wrong.

I had come by now to the latter part of the first quarter of the century and at the same time had arrived at the health clinic. Hiding my smart-phone camera in my right hand, I allowed a good person to open the door for me. (Later on, I would add his interesting face to my album.)

The lobby of course was more than full. I could count at least fifty sick and injured persons in the room and another almost equal number waiting in the hall. I pretended to recognize one of the elderly patients and after a one-person conversation, managed to slip in line behind him. At one time, these people would have been cared for by their *families*; today, they represent fully autonomous taxpayers sans human connections.

I photographed an illegal in a wig, a worn-out specimen demanding unearned benefits. And was I any different? Cursed with the compulsion to look upon life through fractured lenses, I have spent my years on the verge of tears.

With one eye, I tried to continue with the book I had been reading, and with the other managed to stay in line. When both failed, I began dredging up memories of a certain playground experience of seventy years ago. This almost succeeded, except for those dear faces having fallen out of memory and mind. Only dogs, they say, suffer in the way humans do. More than once, I have witnessed Milbrook's hound moaning for his lost mother while in the midst of sleep.

I moved forward three places to take up behind a negro sort of person with an obscene tattoo on his neck. It was clear to me that he had raped a few persons of various genders, but why was I, a person of my attainments, waiting in line with a person of this kind? I tried again to slip forward a few places but was immediately yanked back by this selfsame negro uttering words of extreme vulgarity. I had thought, wrongly, that I was familiar with all such expressions. I grinned boyishly, hoping to ameliorate him. Just then a doctor emerged from the office with his stethoscope and strode toward us with an impatient expression calculated to intimidate people less-well-salaried than himself. I lifted my cane. People like that, they could more easily leap to the moon than intimidate a man like me.

There were others waiting in line, not to ignore a Japanese/Korean/Tibetan or Chinese type with no more right to a place in American society than a koala bear. I trained my gaze on this person, causing him to blush and look away. Very soon now, I would be given my tax-payer-supplied blood-pressure, white corpuscle, and tyrosine kinase receptor tests. My old grandfather! Did ever *that* one concern himself with such matters?

He did not, and yet he could shoot the eyes out of a rattlesnake at forty yards. They understood this, the negroes of that county when they came to vote. And *his* father? I know only this, that in 1864 he came home with three Yankee scalps and one penis—preserved now in formaldehyde—in his knapsack.

I entered the doctor's office in full aplomb, a guileless smile playing about my teeth and lips. The doctor was about what you expected—a business-like professional who might or might not know anything about medicine. In either event, he certainly knew nothing of literature or history or cosmology generally. Me, I know a little bit about everything. He did have an aquarium suffused with green light, a ten-gallon, approximately, container used to incubate his leeches. The "nurse" was also a male—I wanted to puke—whose aplomb was perhaps even more overdeveloped than my own. I was made to complete a questionnaire, a long one, and then given an injection to ward off some of the cooties in circulation then.

"Hm," the doctor reported. "You've put on a few pounds since I last saw you."

"Yes. My metabolism has pretty well shut down."

"We'll have to do something about that."

"No, no, I don't miss it."

(Had only he known about my opinions and reading habits, he would have euthanized me on the spot.) However, I allowed this pair of off-duty lovers to conduct further explorations relative to my kidney, testicles, lungs, and ear canals. The next minutes were used to extract and then replace the catheter plugged into my bladder three weeks previously. An uncomfortable procedure, I was nevertheless grateful for the freedom to walk about the city in dry underwear while leaving naught but nearly-imperceptible stains of urine on the sidewalk. Finished with it, I offered the "nurse" a gratuity which he declined and then sallied out the northside door and phased my way into the madding crowd.

The time had come to return to headquarters; instead, I veered off onto Dietrich Eckhart Street and paced the whole distance to Brooklyn's second-greatest library, said to hold 1.9 million volumes. An appreciable number of tattered youths were loitering on the staircase, intellectuals in beards and shoes. I waded through the midst of them and entered a vestibule hung with oil paintings of Martin Luther King, Jr., and Moses. Right away, I betook myself to the history section on the third floor, carefully evading the professional librarian who detested the sight of me. There was admittedly some fine stuff in this area, including a proportionate number of volumes in the only foreign language I could easily read. After selecting some of the more promising titles, I had chosen to sit on the floor among the books themselves, but then sprang up again when I detected that I had deposited a wee (irony not intended), wee pool of urine in the place. A new title had been added since my last visit, an interpretive history with maps and archeological diagrams regarding the Safavid Dynasty—my sort of stuff.

It was dim in that area of the building, and I was able to ignite a cigarette without notifying the unpleasant librarian. Everyone knows that good prose became unavailable at the close of the nineteenth century; even so, the information I was seeing was as strange and alien to me as the latest findings in quantum physics. This is what I was born for—not for utility and social participation, but for art, beauty, goodness, and information that travels direct to the enjoyment centers of the mind. Which is not to say that others should wish to be like me.

"Small chance of that!" said the proctor, who had come upon me while I was unaware. "Cigarette, too!"

She kicked at me with her low-heel brown shoes.

"No, ma'am!" said I, grinning boyishly. (Someday I would win her over, the bitch.) "No, ma'am, I was just reading up on the Safavid Regime. You know how it is, the way things were in those days."

She softened a tiny bit. I went on:

"The only time when women were actually treated fairly."

I woke to the sound of tugboats at a little past three. Out in the harbor, an oil freighter was docking inch by inch. I had been sleeping, sleeping on a pillow of history books. According to the time, it was twelve past three when finally, I gathered myself and after offering one last small marginal correction to the *Sylloge Nummorum Graecorum* I was using, took the stairs to the second floor, and then the nearest elevator for the rest of the journey. Anyone hoping to track me by way of those little blinking lights on elevator panels would find they had been entirely hoaxed. Coming to rest at ground level, I hesitated three seconds and then burst forth suddenly at high speed, foiling anyone thinking to ambush me. The day was bright and brilliant but much colder than just yesterday. How cold was it? I'm supposed to accompany myself with a thermometer all the time? I had of course forgotten about the little device embedded in my high-cost watch. But even with my glasses, I couldn't read the Japanese.

I moved slowly past the James Earl Ray column, meeting a really gorgeous girl who declined to notice me. I turned and followed. Her skirt was purple and short, my favorite length and color. Further, her impertinent hams (dumplings they seemed) trembled in my favorite way, neither too extravagantly nor the other way around. Took two photos of that. Her hair was alright, too, though lacking that raven-like coloration that keeps me awake at night. In fact, the hair was without much distinction, and her hosiery lacked that seam that in better days used to run from heel to who knows what. Accordingly, I turned about and caught up with my earlier progress on my trek to the barber shop.

It was a bit warmer now I thought, but no it was only a bakery allowing its divine aroma to escape to the outside world. I entered, and how could I not? Save for his glazed expression, the confectioner was a more or less characteristic-looking person for New York City. We evaluated each other.

"Hi," said I.

He turned away. I was old and had snow on the brim of my Afghan cap. Not far away, another customer, a blackamoor of some description, a stickup artist if ever I had seen one, was continually fuddling with what either was a knife or revolver ensconced in his pantaloons. Not wishing at this time to observe a crime taking place in front of my face, I turned and spoke slowly in dialect:

"I have it—why not let me buy you something? It's cold outside and Christmas is hard by."

He spun toward me with a ferocious face but then quickly relented and returned the implement to his pocket.

"Yo, pecker," he quoth, grinning in the way they have.

And so we stood by, we twain, while the six-foot-four entity went about pointing out the goods he chiefly desired. It cost me, this affair, some thirty dollars and a fair amount more. Not wanting to spend yet more money on such entities, I returned to the highroad, entered the throng, and stepped at a commensurate speed among the shoppers, striving to protect my toes from the high heels and knurled boots of those traveling at my side. I crossed a world of intersections and a quantity of alleys with individuals in them. I halted to view a kiosk offering the sort of tourist merchandise we New Yorkers despise. That was when a woman of some kind trod on my right foot with a metal heel that acuminated to a point. I yelled at her before choosing not to and instead hobbled to the curb, beseated myself, and worked on my foot. The bitch must have weighed more than the town's premier linebacker. I did have my Glock, but she would have been far away by that time.

The next barber shop was uninviting diversity-wise, wherefore I crossed to the opposite shore of the street engulphed now in late-afternoon shadow. I was attracted to a pet shop full of adorable little puppies and was able to agitate the little girl standing next to me by drawing my piece and aiming at them. Meantime, my catheter had snarled, and some part of the fluid was draining down my leg. I jumped into the next-door dress shop and while sheltering my face against the CCTV cameras, moved hastily to the men's facility—they hadn't any—before then jumping into the ladies' room. There was but one lady in the place, and her revulsion was caused more by my visage than by my member I believe. Coming to the sink, I quickly extracted the catheter, a more painful operation than you might have expected, and then voided my lopsided bladder at tedious length. A shopper dressed in a bargain hat entered but then immediately turned and went out again. I do of course realize that I am no longer the winsome youth of female dreams, but I am not fully as awful-looking as some have allowed themselves to believe. Wishing to elude the police, I exited at once and hid amid the crowd.

I trod for blocks, coming at last to a suitable barber shop and first-aid facility with but one chair which I preempted immediately. His own haircut, the barber's, was none too encouraging, but then I don't suppose he had inflicted it upon himself. He smiled, if that's what it was, and then presented me an album showing different hair styles. Never before had I been given a choice such as this. Wanting value for money, I inspected the photos with care, settling finally upon Errol Flynn, a 1950s personality said to have resembled me. Once I had finished with the album, it was my intention to sleep through the operation. I was drowsy, and my day's vitality was moving to its end.

From my chair, I could see numbers of ordinary people abandoning their office buildings and then congregating at the entrances to the bars and subway stations. I saw a sick man, as pale and peaked as you'd ever want to see, still "bringing home the bacon," as the bourgeoisie say. Thirty-six years in the same air-conditioned office building, he saw himself as among the earth's most favored. I wanted to go out there, kick him in the ass, and carry him as hurriedly as possible to the nearest mortuary.

I did sleep briefly but then immediately awoke and leapt up when the barber set about amputating that little wart under my chin. It was painful, believe me, and the blood ran profusely over my collar and tie. I could not remember the dream I had been enjoying, a multicolor affair with stars and green fields.

"Goddamn it! That hurts!" I admitted,

"Are you going to sit down and let me clean up that mess? Or not?"

I sat. The tie was ruined, and without permission, the barber removed it and tossed it in the biologic waste container. Slowly and slowly, it was turning dark outside; winter it was, and mercifully the days were growing shorter. Short, dark, and cold, my favorite weather. It restricts the ignorant, some of them, to their quarters and gives free play to those who see more clearly when the masses are out of view. That was the moment the surgeon stopped his work.

"Curfew," he reported.

"What?"

"Curfew. It's six o'clock."

"Goddam it! What sort of 'curfew' are we talking about here?"

"Where do you live?"

I described my neighborhood's location.

"You're already late then. Sixty-five, please."

"What?"

"Sixty-five dollars. Don't forget your coat."

I did pay, not without complaint, however. He was and no doubt still is larger than me, and I'm conspicuously older. Peeved almost beyond endurance, I handed over a starched hundred-dollar bill and idiotically accepted the piffling amount of change he offered. He then ushered me to the door and nudged me out into the cold dark world.

He had spoken the truth about six o'clock. The buses were running, and the faces on display almost made me feel sorry for them. Night comes early in these canyons where nightlife commences immediately after lunch. The crepuscule turns shop windows into mirrors, allowing me to see my haircut in detail. Nor had the blood entirely ceased. On that showing, I dared not seek for public toilets along the way, no matter how clogged my intubation. Needing a drink, I nevertheless declined to enter the next saloon that came my way. My bloody shirt might summon the police who would see that I was "out-of-precinct" at this untoward hour. Therefore, I plodded on, trying hard to make my gait like a generic person's.

Came five-thirty, and I was no nearer to the hostel than about a mile and a quarter. I ambled past a triangular structure said to be the meeting place of a Pythagorean cult. We call this squeezed area the *Defile of Nihilism*, those of us. Here, thousands of windows look down on the town, many holding faces in them. I refused to light a cigarette at this intersection, not with a policeman only half a block distant. All too late, I realized it were that same policeman who adored opals.

"Hey, big buddy!" he declared. "What'cha got in that mouth of yours?"

I spit it out onto the sidewalk, the half-inch stub of a moistened cigarette that right away rolled off into the snow where it would be impossible to relight it.

"Still prowling around at six-twelve in the afternoon? I think we got a problem here."

"No, no; I just wanted some waffles and buttermilk. But that bitch waitress wouldn't give me any!"

"Bitch with red hair?"

"Why, yes."

"Big ass on her?"

"Exactly!"

"Okay, I'll have a talk with her when she gets home."

He was not unkind. Too, his tie clasp had a ruby in it, a manufactured item far too large to be authentic.

"Those old manufacturers, they can do just about anything nowadays," I offered. "They can even make artificial women!"

"With big asses and red hair? Don't knock it just because you don't got one."

We laughed riotously. He had a high school ring and a pot belly.

"Well, reckon I'd better be moving on," the author said.

"Yeah. You're way out of your precinct, and it's almost six-fifteen. I ought to run you in."

I laughed in comradely fashion, smiled, turned, and then hobbled off at my best speed. The man was ignorant and overweight, and his enormous feet had become entangled in the thong of his nightstick.

The next hundred yards were not so bad, at the end of which I jumped into one of those stores and retired to the men's toilet. An elderly man, as old almost as me, was moaning in one of the cells.

"Hi, there!" he said cheerfully. "Say, you couldn't hand me some toilet paper, could you? There ain't any in here."

Idiot. Certainly, I could have provided him toilet paper. Instead, I corrected my catheter and then peed at length. The last I needed at this point was a bowel movement with just one toilet in the whole place and no paper anywhere. Admit it, your great cities don't acknowledge old men's excretory needs. On the other hand, the city is crawling with youths able to go for days and days.

The store itself was grander than my hometown. I dawdled down aisle 37, testing some of the digital products of mysterious usages. The clerk was a red-headed woman (big ass), who already loathed the sight of me.

"Are you trained in the usages of these appliances?" I asked peremptorily.

She began to pale.

"Well, we had a workshop, and I got an 'A' in it."

"Excellent. And who, may I ask, was the instructor? Steve?"

"Well, he was real tall. Not real, real tall, but pretty tall."

"Wonderful. And did he get into the equations? You can't go far without the equations."

"I've only been here a couple of weeks!"

"Ah. Could I just see your I.D. please? No, take it out of your purse please."

She was nervous. No doubt she was and is a single mother with a bunch of illegal babies to feed. Red-headed Negresses are few and far apart, but with them, large asses are standard equipment. Working slowly, she removed and then passed over to me a membership card in the "Woke" organization. I was much nearer to her than I wanted to be, but she at least was using an effective perfume.

"Very well," I said, relenting. "But next time, I'll be asking about the equations."

She agreed. It needed me several minutes to find the manager and complain about the wench.

Outside, the streets were dark and sinister as were the people. Pulling my hat low, I continued my homeward trek. In former days, the curfew couldn't identify a person from his genomic badge alone. Ahead, I spotted a hulking figure spotlighted by a streetlamp, his egg-shaped head telling all I wanted to know about *his* genome. I turned to the right, passed down a long driveway, and placed myself in an alley that ran behind the office buildings. The usual black cats known to us from literature were absent, however. Even here, there was danger all about. I moved past a drunken person drawn up in the fetal position. The chill was godawful and wouldn't have been tolerated in my own southern hometown. I spit on it.

Soon, I emerged from the alley but then turned and went back again. Every intersection had a large person stationed in the penumbra of each streetlamp. Knowing what happens to people like me at the hands of people like that, I hailed the next taxi—"next" was twenty-seven minutes later—and leapt inside. The conveyance held one person already (two if we consider the driver and three if you consider me), but I could not immediately measure his quality. His pate was three-fourths shaved, and the two wings of his extraordinary moustache came together behind his head. Said this person:

"Don't worry about me bro. I don't put no stock in that *curfew,* so-called."

"But *I* do," the driver contributed. A stodgy type, he was using his quantum phone to call headquarters. Smaller in girth than a pencil, the device had a laser beam that fixed on me.

The driver, a good man in spite of everything else, slowed to let me out. Even so, I almost fell on my face from the momentum that comes from abandoning a vehicle moving at just ten miles per hour or even less. My cane fell to the pavement, ejecting the blade that now lay in full view. A hulking sort of person stood guard at the intersection. I snuffed out my cigarette and, putting on a cheerful expression, managed to work my way past her without creating a disturbance. It was late, I was old, and still had far to go.

Five

Far to go, yes, but I was in need of coffee and mayhap a dram of brandy as well. In accord with that, I diverged some two blocks to that tin-like structure mentioned earlier where a person should be able to have a drink without being recruited to hear other peoples' stories. By my standards, the night was young as yet, and my vitality had put on new growth. I was humming as I strode, only somewhat intimidated by a gristly New York cityscape inset with millions of eyes. To leap forward in the narrative, I did arrive at that metallic-grey building and threw myself inside before anyone might see that I was "out of curfew."

The lobby was pleasing, a capacious area with green sofas and a curved mahogany bar that must have extended for twenty, possibly twenty-five yards before doubling back on itself. The bartenders were bald, some of them, and had all the same noncommittal facial expressions. The orchestra was playing a moonlight piece of piano and cello, and the artwork was bad. This was no ordinary rough-and-tumble meeting place for CFOs, political candidates, equity brokers, Fortune 500 consultants, and the like. Nor, on the contrary, was it fit for the sort of decent people one used to find. I huddled over my cherry daiquiri wearing a sophisticated expression that seemed to say that nothing I had ever done had ever been outside my personal experience. I smoked, called for another drink, and began to reminisce about certain historical events of personal interest.

The restroom, if possible, was even more luxurious than the lobby and represented a tremendous promotion over the very best room in my old hometown of 1948. I detected a pair of feet, both in shoes, beneath the door of one of the cells.

"Howdy," I remarked, pretty certain I'd get no response. I washed then and combed and wasted a minute reviewing my face in the well-beveled mirror. They're right, them as declare that men are evil. Not perhaps as evil as those blasé women sitting on their preposterous orifices in the over-decorated lobby. I fluffed my iron-grey hair, decanted half an hour's worth of urine into the golden sink, and then went out to join the clientele at the bar. This time, I ordered stronger stuff but had to dig deep to come up with the fee in dimes, quarters, and two red pennies. Rich people are calm, and why should they not be? They don't have to get up in the morning, and their purses are full of paper money. That was the moment I detected a reasonable-looking person sitting at a distance from me who with his eyes and that certain nobility in the shape of his head, reminded me of me.

"Howdy," I started to say before then stifling myself in case he didn't wish to speak, a normal reaction among deep people. Instead, I slithered two seats in his direction and with my liquor tilted for consumption, stared seriously at the myriad of interesting-looking wine and whiskey bottles arrayed like bowling pins behind the bar. I focused on one label particularly, a hexagonal business with the image of a sailing ship on the high seas. I determined to have a drink of that before I left.

"Howdy," he said.

"Hello. Strange, isn't it, how people like us can recognize each other."

"Indeed."

"The furrowed brow. A battered book sticking out of a person's coat pocket."

"And about . . . what? Seventy-five years old?"

"Seventy-eight," I admitted ruefully. I also gave him my real name.

"Never expected to find someone like you in this dreadful place."

I came closer. His nose was a problem, and he had more wattle than a person likes to see; even so, he had several of the distinctive marks that make one distinctive. "And you," I put in, "how do *you* happen to be here?"

"I own it."

"Love the décor."

We laughed, one of us. The pores of his nose were so large a mite had nested in one of them. He edged closer to me, got into his glasses, and jumped back suddenly.

"What are you, some kind of goddamn curfew violator for Christ's sakes? Close the door when you leave, Okay? Look, we just aren't in the market for people like you. Not tonight and not tomorrow either."

"Wednesday?"

He withdrew the book from my right-side pocket, scrutinized the cover (his eyes were not much better than his nose) and then read out loud a sentence or two.

"Ah, man! This stuff is just pure shit. You think you're going to fix America with this shit? Pure shit, that's what it is."

"You have to read the whole thing."

"The hell I do!"

"Okay, just the first chapter."

"You're sick, man." He called the bartender, who came with alacrity, and then required him to pour me a drink from that bottle with the ship on it. The orchestra had started up, and some of the Jews were dancing to it, old women in pricy gowns, unhappy and fat, their faces coagulated with wealth and sin. They really were appalling, as I mentioned to the owner.

"They really are appalling, aren't they?"

"Kind of slow, aren't you?"

"But think what we could do, you and me. Me with my brains and you with your wealth."

"You're crazy as hell! What kind of brains?"

"What kind of wealth?"

"I need to piss."

"Not nearly as much as me."

Taking my drink with me, we raced to the facility, a thousand-square-foot arena supplied with toilets in a row and a very great many bars of pale green soap. So, this then is how a civilization dies, not with a whimper but bars of perfumed soap shaped like women. We urinated at length, another competition in which I had to admit defeat. His bladder was larger than his head, and his head wasn't all that small to begin with.

He took me to the roof of his extravagant building and proceeded to point our other properties mortgaged to him in the surrounding district. Suddenly, we ducked down to get out of view of another elderly person scanning us with field glasses from a rooftop of her own. The night was proceeding, and the snow, gritty as sand, was flecking the lenses of our glasses, his and mine.

"Well!" said I after another minute, "I really need to get going. They'll be sending people to look for me!"

"Seriously doubt that. And don't be thinking you're going to walk out of here with that glass. First, you don't pay for the brandy, second, you try to swipe the goddamn glass!"

I drew the thing from my jeans and handed it over to him, a difficult maneuver at this altitude. I much needed to piss, but the wind you understand. The building was comprised of fourteen floors, and the stairs on this occasion had two discrete, or rather one discrete and two indiscrete individuals impeding the path. I stepped over a growling escrubilator who, exhausted after its long climb, had geared down to semi-animation.

Six

Bus service had stopped, and it wasn't till past eight that I got myself home again. Two of the derelicts were fighting in the hall, and I had to go quickly to my own rooms to take a leak. Gnawing on the other man's ear, Lathrop was bleeding from an icepick lodged in his upper arm. Two of the transgendered residents had meantime drifted down from the fourth floor and, holding hands, were ever and again giggling at the action. It was shocking to me that so much blood could come from so tiny a wound. Apparently, the weapon had found an important artery, and Lathrop's predicament was becoming a real embarrassment. I whispered encouragement to both combatants, though it did seem to me that Marcus' advantage would prove dispositive before much longer.

My belongings had *not* been disturbed, and I was able to read half a chapter in Edward Halle's *The Union of Two Noble and Illustre Famelies* (1548) before slipping into bed and dialing my radio to that Tulsa station where the common people were invited to express their opinions. At such a distance, the station was weak and often interrupted by voices from elsewhere in the space-time continuum. Truth is, I have always preferred your old-time *tube* radios that allow a person to witness, as it were, the pulsing of the rays coming at you. I despise all efforts to hide the complexity of things. As with a medium-quality escrubilator, the human body is hundreds of times more complicated than seen by your ordinary portrait painter.

I went on reading, or tried so to do in the midst of screaming from the outer hall. Contrary to my prediction, Marcus had given up and gone away, a weakling without the bowels to pursue things to their end. Came 9:27, I switched off the lamp, and in spite of the nasal sound of Blephy once again droning on at long length about his terminal orgasm, tried to sleep.

It was a turbid night with high winds and "ghosts," as it seemed, slithering past my oblong window. New Yorkers—I admit it—can endure anything, and I could perceive a representative struggling against the wind down in the street below. What did they want actually? Higher wages to pay for outrageous real estate prices? They should be more like me, who has a reason for being here.

Hell, I could just lie here for hours reveling in this stuff. But lately, I say, my taste has rotated over to *Mughal art*, based upon my liking for it. Sitting up in bed, I trained my flashlight on that famous portrait of Jahangir sniffing at a flower held to his flared nose.

Now once again fully awake, I turned on the radio and dialed to an Irish station that must have been extraordinarily powerful to cross so many miles of ocean. The speaker was despicable, judging from his accent, but on the other hand his interpretation of the news comported very largely with my own. In the Irish-English conflict, he held with the Celts, while in other matters he appeared to have accepted my view of a considerable number of things.

There were other voices at the extreme edge of the

dial, and I was able (barely) to pick up scads of odd languages and even, occasionally, a momentary silence caused by obstructions coming between the sources and me. Such a privilege—I could lie on my belly in my excellent bed and make an effortless tour (speaking figuratively) of my little slice of the galactic "pie."

I had thought the tumult in the hall had ended, but instead of that I was shaken at that moment by a loud cry of pain emitted from just outside my door. Rousing myself, I got into my shoes, urinated, and went to the toilet. I found just three persons in the hall, one of them a modified individual from the fourth floor, (where else?) who had gathered up a fistful of Lathrop's goiter and was squeezing it pitilessly. Although I try never to involve myself in the affairs of ordinary people, I stepped from my doorway and yelled out loud and clear:

"Hey! That's not good, what you're doing."

But the malefactor went on pressing my friend's abnormality. I actually wanted to strike the blighter but lacked any sort of instrument. You are asking about the third person mentioned above? He had exited to stage right the moment he saw my exacerbated face.

Returning to my sanctuary, I read a few pages more and then fell into a disturbed sleep. From outside, the normative sounds of nighttime New York had penetrated my cell, and I was further aggrieved by that moth or whatever it was now thrashing about inside my doorknob. Reluctantly, I retrieved my phone and ignoring the time of day, dialed Forrest's number, Forrest Chorn, whose housemaid finally answered.

"Yes?"

She sounded drowsy.

"Hi. You sound drowsy," I explained.

"Who is this?"

"May I speak to Forrest?"

"Forrest is dead! Died two years ago."

"Not necessarily. If you knew him as I know him . . ."

She hung up the phone on me. Dismayed, I called again, this time reaching neither Forrest nor his assistant. It was eleven o'clock, and my diurnal allotment of energy had, as it were, reinstantiated itself. At the same time, my television, maintained always at low volume, was offering a series of commercial advertisements featuring a yellow giraffe promoting a brand of toothpaste, a girl in a small bathing suit, and a pair of wide-eyed cats singing about a brand of beer. Never let it be imagined that our country had failed to pick up where the Greeks left off.

Turning away from television, I alternated over to radio, a higher medium by far. I found a station in Binghamton, a hundred-thousand-watt facility that somehow had broken through the carapace that shuts New York off from the normal world. But were the advertisements any better here, and was there any hope of narrowing in on an episode of *Sky King* or *Jack Armstrong, the All-American Boy*?

I repaired to the toilet and among other procedures gazed into the lying mirror. From near and far, I could hear ambulances and police cars carrying out their functions. A fire had broken out in Queens, an oddly-named district famous for its hairdressers, and from my window I could perceive a deal of black smoke occluding the moon on that side. My excitement increased. For up-to-date information, I was alternately employing my radio, computer, and escrubilator. Just then, the great iron bells of the Fifth Avenue Antinomian Temple began laboring portentously, a God-like noise with an eighty-mile radius. I changed channels, stumbling upon another iteration of that ad for Elmer Foib's new novel. Surrendering to my second-favorite delusion, I envisioned great balls of fire targeting New York City, the financial district especially, shareholders with their hair falling out and me with the funds I had so percipiently transferred to Italy. I envisioned the 47-yard optical telescope over in Suffolk County working frenziedly to pinpoint the danger. Tumescent by now, I changed over to my stronger glasses and clove to the window, striving with limited success to peer through the smoke and rain. There were eleven other floors above me in this special building of mine, and I was ensured, so to speak, against rain doing harm to my papers and things. Under these conditions, I chose to revisit the hall and learn what my friends were doing.

Taw was sleeping while Lathrop was weeping softly over the harm to his goiter. Neither seemed much alarmed either by the weather or increasing possibility of cosmic events. We were all of us old men and except for me had grown indifferent to impending disaster. Me, I yearned for it.

"You're an alarmist," said Gliese, Bill Gliese, putting aside his newspaper and using my name. "What, you're afraid of some sort of impending disaster or something?"

"On the contrary."

Percy, much disheveled, emerged from his chamber, retrieved a cup of coffee, deposited himself on the green leather sofa, and then, as was his wont, began probing the cushions for lost coins. Formerly the heir to a digital fortune, he was by now the impecuniest man in the building.

"Lend me a dollar?" he asked.

"Sure." I paid, my eyes on Dwayne who also was wont to badger me for loans. I have already dealt with this one in an earlier paragraph (not shown here) and no longer felt I owed him anything. And then, too, he had a heavy brow, and his nostrils were so flared that one, or more than one actually, could see halfway to his

brains. Never an admirer of human physiology, I had
other complaints as well.

Outside, the weather had begun snowing again.
Pressing at the window, we witnessed New Yorkers in
automobiles hurrying back and forth to locations far
and near and mid-distance. Impossible not to laugh.
What did they want really? To be there instead of here?
Suddenly, a blue and grey car of some description
slipped in the snow and ran direct into a large red vehicle full of odious youths. We watched transfixed as four
of these last-named individuals exited hurriedly and
began examining the damage to their adored conveyance. And did my ole great-grandfather ever fret himself over *his* car? He never had one.

But this was nothing as compared to the policeman,
a ruddy man with hat and jowls who seemed actually to
be trying to adjudicate the matter in a more or less fair-
minded fashion. New York policemen? I see them as
the town's highest-ranking citizens destined for para-
dise when their time comes around. Let me be one of
these, and I'd have slain fifty miscreants before the first
anniversary of my hiring date.

"Shoot 'em!" I yelled in reference to the half-dozen
pedestrians and passengers dithering at the scene." You
can do it!"

"They won't," said Percy, speaking realistically. "But
if he" (the policeman) "did, he'd have to spend the next
fifty years just doing paperwork."

He was right. In these decadent days, the country
preferred to slobber over perpetrators than to shoot
them. I touched my revolver.

"Put it back," said Marcus using my name. "You
couldn't hit 'em anyway."

"What did you say?"

"Hit 'em. Good God man, you can't even lift a spoon-
ful of sugar without spilling it all over the tablecloth!"

"You say that? Why, I could . . ."

But that was when a second mishap took place at the intersection, this time entailing a bright-yellow taxicab and a fat woman wriggling on the pavement.

"A Jew!" I shouted. "A palpable Jew!"

"Oh, shut up. You don't know that."

Right away, the policeman dashed over to help her, effectively sealing her off from any bullet of mine.

But soon, the snow had covered the blood, and the cars had all been towed away. We men had gone back to our sofas and chairs and were each thinking a person's own thoughts. Blephy was smoking on a Turkish pipe as large as a saxophone, fomenting an outpouring of blue smoke that filled the hall to a depth. It had become necessary to stand if we wished to breathe.

"Good leaf," said Percy politely. "Egyptian?"

"Hemp. Pure hemp."

"And you'll be using it all night long I suppose?"

He never answered, Blephy, and we were too tired and old to continue the matter.

Seven

I slept for about eleven discontinuous hours and then awoke to see my stocks had gained some twelve thousand dollars in notional value. My friends out in the hall, what did they know about money and the antinomian insights that follow in its train? According to official records, I was poor, desperate even, but here I was in this pathetic building thinking thoughts that would have paralyzed the social worker who visited me once each six weeks. She was a pretty entity, though her eyes were too far apart. *There's always something*, something to keep perfection out of reach.

"How have we been making out?" she asked. Her lips were cherry-red and her teeth equally good. She had good skin, too, some of it.

"Oh, not too awful," I replied. I had put away my computers, my microscope, my escrubilator, and camera obscura lest she detect how prosperous I am and was. My closet, too, was empty in case she peeped inside. A mismatched pair of socks lay in view.

Continuing with it, I revealed that "my gout has come back however."

"Well, that's not good. Are you seeing anyone about it?"

She had fine legs, and her hose were taut and shiny. I could envision but could not actually view the assumed garter straps that held them up. All that paraphernalia to entice the eye to the ugliest orifice in nature.

"No, it wouldn't do no good anyhow. It's too late for me. I just need to set here and be patient."

A drop of salt water, a small one, appeared in the corner of her left eye. She, who had never read one-tenth the books I had read, was full of compassion for *me*. If only she had arisen and gone to check the closet, I could have purloined her credit card; instead, I offered her a blunt.

In the afternoon, the snow came back for the ninth time this winter. I welcomed it in the hope that it might cover the blackened snows of yesterday. I look upon the stuff as a sort of insulation to help muffle the noise of New Yorkers castigating each other in the outside streets. I realize that I haven't yet explained why I live in this place.

I live in this place so as more easily to confound the New York Stock Exchange and grow wealthy. "Take the smallest possible risk," Taw had urged, "and learn from main-chancers. To grow rich through effort is simply a slight of hand practiced by opportunists mostly. Don't be like that. Learn how to arbitrage the short-selling of currency futures; *that's* the real stuff."

I spent a while in the pages of Golding's *A Briefe Discourse of the Murthur of G. Saunders* and then returned to the hall now almost empty. Percy's door had been left ajar, his unpleasant body stretched out on the bed in his underwear. We are old men, all of us, and must rely upon the pity of social workers, the last truly naïve people in America. Taking a seat next to this man's seeming corpse, I again questioned silently why old men choose to go on living. His ear was uncovered, and I was easily able to drop inside it the still-wriggling roach I had been conserving in my cigarette case for the past two days. God, his feet were ugly, and his legs vermiculated with varicose veins. I wait with increasing impatience for men, cultivated men, to be transformed into high-grade quantum machines. This man, I admit, did have a particular knowledge of North American geology and associated things. Grandchildren he also had, one of them a more or less decent human being who shared with me his subscription to my favorite eugenics journal. Give me twenty years, and I might have turned him into something more or less like me.

It was and is my compulsion to take day-and-night excursions through New York City whether I wish it or not. We maintain, us men, good relations with the Police Department for which reason we have been urged to submit written eyewitness descriptions of the city's Negroes and their behavior. Given fifty dollars for each plausible report, some of my hallmates are now much better able to pay their expenses. An enormous area, New York is overflowing with clues of all sorts offering good rewards to those who know how to harvest them. And so tonight, once again, I got into my Marlon Brando jacket, my Glock, my tin of blunts and other cigarettes, and scurried out into the cold black weather. Christmas was drawing nigh, and I was unwilling to

ignore the amazing decorations hoisted by the adher-
ents of that risible faith. I passed a shoe repair exuding
a haze of green and yellow neon and after twenty steps,
turned and came back to stand in the midst of it. Like
methamphetamine are bright colors to me. Strength
returning, I entered the place and went to advise the
shoemaker himself, a rough-looking quantity who
could have been of real service to the Confederacy.
Taking my revolver from its unspecified place, I put it
down in front of him and awaited his reaction.

"Hm. Give you a hundred dollars for it."

"Blimey!" I pronounced. "I paid *six* times that!"

He gathered it gingerly and aimed it in turn at four
or five pedestrians ambling ignorantly past his shop. A
.357 magnum produces more than enough noise to
have put him out of business. He was about to return
to his work when I spoke up:

"I need a holster for that thing. A lubricated holster
that attaches to my belt and runs down my trouser leg
on the left side."

"My uncle was lefthanded. But *he* used a shoulder
holster."

"A good man, your uncle?"

"Oh, hell yes! Till they gave him that injection."

I stood by as he measured and then began snipping
out the leather pattern the project required. He was
slow and competent and if not as muscular as a weight-
lifter, he was about 75% that way. In my imagination, I
saw him singlehandedly lifting iron balls and inserting
then gingerly into Confederate cannon ware. I paid him
(too much) for his work and for the yellow holster that
now comprises my newest accessory. And then I went
outside, stood in the blaze of holiday lights, and drew
my gun four times at lightning speed. Deep down, I
knew I'd never use it.

I am and was tired and old and have outlived my

formative time. Were it not better my friends and I took ship to the sun and contribute to the life-giving combustion for which that place is so famous? Not quite yet.

I plodded on, smoking two successive cigarettes in plain open view. My sexual apparatus may be more or less useless by now, but my revolver is not. I moved past a public gymnasium wherein a dozen narcissists were disporting themselves in shiny clothing. A woman was worried about her belly, her boyfriend by contrast focusing on his abs, pecs, and pecker. In all this world, there's not a single mammal, fish, or reptile as self-fixated as this. Bringing my Will into play, I refused to vomit at this time.

Another cigarette and two hundred yards further, I came upon a delicatessen still doing at this late hour. The proprietor, a Jew of some strain, looked up at me with silent hatred. I immediately took out a few hundred-dollar bills and allowed him to gaze upon them. His assistant, transparently a mischling, was dressed in a blood-stained apron held by a string. He did not—and I hesitate to say it—did *not* look altogether kosher to me.

"A pound of chittlings," I demanded. "A mess of collards and half a peck of cornmeal if you please."

He paled and sputtered.

"You come in here? Some kind of *noodge*? What am I, a doormat? You want I should call my brother!"

I could have drawn my revolver but didn't. If only I could rewrite the bylaws of evolution! He was six inches smaller than me but had consumed so many blintzes and gefilte fishes that I disdained engaging with him at just this time. And then, too, there was that other person who would have relished a chance at my pore old head.

More and more these days, I feel that I've been

transported to a science-fiction planet where every
good and decent thing has become illegal. Chastise a
negro and end up in jail. Compliment a woman and
end up in prison. Discontinue a kike and . . .

I stopped. Not ten yards in front of me, a 300-pound
negro with an egg-shaped head was strolling hand-in-
hand with a palpable white girl of above-average good
looks. That nauseous feeling that I had so often felt before now swept over me like a weather condition. My
grandfather, why was he never where he most was
needed? This time, I really did draw my revolver but
then had to waste some time disentangling the thing
from what I had believed to be the holster. In the
meanwhile, another couple even worse than the cited
one had come up from behind and was nudging me
faster than at my age I am easily able to go. Infuriated,
chagrined, and in other ways displeased, I spun on this
prototypical pair and gained a fair amount of pleasure
from the expression on their faces when they perceived
the outlet of my .357 pressed tightly to their navels.
They yelped. But did the author of this memoir have
the presence to squeeze the trigger? You knew in ad-
vance that he did not.

I wandered far, pretty far, and then appeared before
a late-night bar-and-restaurant of which the town has
so many. Though lacking in diversity, I entered and
positioned myself by habit where I could view as much
as possible while being viewed in return by as few as
possible. The place itself, encircled in yellow tape, held
all manner of New York types even if from a distance
the crowd might almost have been mistaken for normal
people with their wives and others. Coming forward to
claim a place, I capsized the spittoon, a brass object full
of immiscible things. Having at last beseated myself at
a child-size table not much larger than a frisbee, I
plunged for a cigarette, ignited it, and sucked on it

twice. I had wanted a more elevated table whence I could more properly enjoy this array of twenty-first-century lesbians, immigrants, abolitionists, and transgendered varieties generally. My old grandfather! I called for a post-modern Flood to cover the earth; instead, the waiter, conspicuously a northern Yankee, presented me a menu with a great many French-language words on it. He himself was pale, this waiter, and closely resembled another such person I had seen at one time. Old as I am, I could have thrashed to death this instantiation with my handkerchief. Or could have so done when I was marginally younger.

The place was full of clues, but for the nonce I accepted the water he offered, drank most of it, and let fall my smoldering cigarette into the residue. It displeased him. I lit another. I was dressed just well enough that he couldn't be sure I wasn't an important person, mayhap a consultant or broker or even a public relations person. I invited his eye to settle on the grip of my revolver that stood just within his line of vision. I would have preferred the female waitress three tables away, a healthy-looking Italianate with surly lips and pronounced buttocks. If she were wearing panties, as likely she was, they would be tight, white, and moist. I grinned wildly at her, but she never saw.

In the fulness of time, I was served a porcelain bowl carrying an excelsior salad with black olives, anchovies, artichoke hearts, snails, and related material of that kind. Given, too, was I, a blue cheese dressing that cheered me only too excessively perhaps. And so, there was I, sitting where much worse people more rightly belonged.

The salad could not endure for long in face of my need wherefore I turned my notice to other corners of the enormous room. I saw a middle-aged lecher spoon-feeding his attractive secretary and next to that, two analysts, or consultants, or members of advisory committees wasting time before the next shuttle to somewhere. This gorgeous civilization. How long O God, before a contingent of new-age Spartans sweeps it all away?

I took two capsules and tried to calm myself. The lamb chops were good, though for the price I could have bought ten times as many from the grocery store. They had of course been basted in wine, perhaps a whole twelve cents worth. My best all-time meal had comprised three frankfurters cooked on a stick in the woods behind my father's house. The trees—how well I remember them—were full of vampires at that time, and my tent had a hole in it. Lacking danger, the world lacks pleasure.

I turned to view several little 250-pound negro starvelings pressing at the window. Working slowly, I opened wide my maw, inserted about two-thirds of a wine-soaked chop, and proceeded studiously to masticate the object down to dust. This I followed with more wine and a hefty wedge of apple pie with cheese on top. I was at the same time being viewed unfavorably by a table of three post-modern women, careerists, to judge by their apparel, exposing the exact same facial expression so often seen on people addicted to bad smells. I smiled at them, licking my lips in a way just short of breaking the law. Their skirts were remarkably short, of course, proving beyond a doubt just how up-to-date their social affinities were. They wore some jewelry, not too much and not too little but just the right amount precisely. Their make-up was just right, too, just enough to make them, say, about 20% prettier than they were. My old grandmother! She could make buttermilk biscuits (not to mention watermelon-rind pickles) six times better than anything in their collective resumes. And in short, I wanted to slay the lot of them.

I ordered further pie, smoked two cigarettes—none dared challenge me—and then read about six pages in Francis Quarles' leather-bound *Argalus and Parthenia* (1629). There was still a good deal of tumult in and about the entrance of the café owing to the yellow tape, and I calculated I might be able to escape without paying. Outside, an ambulance sped to the entrance followed by a police van and a Lincoln Town Car holding two journalists and a lawyer. Content with my meal, I drained off the last of the coffee and then hobbled up to the cashier entranced, apparently, by the aftermath of the crime in front of her working station.

"I need to get out there!" I explained. "And see if I can help!"

She nodded. She was blond and dull, and her eyes operated like camera shutters widening and closing.

The night was chilly certainly, but the continuous snow had for the most part covered the blood. Five useless policemen were standing about wishing for something to do. I could have helped them with that, had I but had the nerve; instead, I turned westward and began ambulating cheerfully toward Queens, a famous district that lies over and against my own.

An enormous time had gone by since last I had crossed over into this mysterious borough named after a famous troupe of ballet dancers. But the path was miles in length, and to preserve my lapsing energy, I haled down a blue-and-green taxicab with an extraordinarily long antenna fluctuating in the wind. The driver was slow to stop for me while in addition to that, two other individuals could be seen hunkered in the back seat. Even so, I climbed aboard and smiling cordially, fitted my corpse into the little space still available.

"The next person," I suggested cheerfully, "will have to ride on top!"

The taxicab stopped. We were at an intersection,

and already a line of cars had begun honking at us to move forward. The driver turned. He was *not* a natural-born American, that much was immediately clear.

"Hey, mon, I got four little babies to feed, you feel? I gots to have all the suckers I can git! What, *you* want to ride on top?"

"Not really. No."

The oncoming traffic was dense for this or for any hour, and the headlights sporadically illuminated the faces of my traveling companions. One seemed to be a woman and the other a man, a fine distinction in New York City Town. I offered to shake with the nearest one, who jumped back out of range.

"Are we in Queens yet?" I asked politely.

The vehicle stopped. The buildings were gorgeously arrayed with Christmas decorations, and again I questioned why the world could not always be this way.

"Because it just can't!" the passenger furthest from me explained. "And besides, you'd get bored with it."

"Oh? Oh? I don't get bored with Wagner."

"Wagner! Wagner was a racist!"

The taxi stopped again. It was a bleak area, and I realized that I'd have to wait a long time for another ride. With mixed feelings, I abandoned the car with my money intact and alit at the corner of Second Avenue and Jacob's Ladder, filled with wonder that a boy like me could have ended up in a place like this. I smoked and dawdled, filaments of world literature slipping in and out of mind until 11:48 when I was at last accepted by a green-colored taxi piloted by an abbreviated man wearing a paisley tie.

"Whew," I said. "I wasn't sure anyone would pick me up!"

"Me neither."

"Because of how I'm dressed?"

"You're okay."

"That last fellow . . ."

"Drives that green and blue job?"

"Blue and green actually."

"I'm going to kill that son-of-a-bitch someday! He talks to niggers, takes them places."

I said no more. He had a tiny photograph no larger than two square inches affixed to his sun visor. Such was the ignorance of history in this city, I doubt one in a thousand could recognize the handsome face of Corneliu Codreanu. He was a good driver, too, this brief man with protuberant eyes and ears of unlike size.

"Are we in Queens yet?" I asked. (I had said that I would say no more, a lie as it turned out.)

"Hmm?"

"Are we in Queens yet?"

"We'll know when we get there, don't you think? Anyway, I'm not licensed in Queens."

"I see. Well, maybe if you could just stop and let me out, I . . ."

"Stop? At this speed? That would be the end of you and me both, for Christ's sakes."

"I see."

Lacking liquor, I had only cigarettes to calm me. The Christmas decorations, previously so beautiful to my mind, had deteriorated into an ambiguated whorl. As we sped past them. I saw last-moment shoppers frozen in space with one foot off the ground. Such is the effect of speed on human perception. According to Einstein indeed, mass increases exponentially as one nears light speed. That was when I had the presence to turn and find that we were being chased resolutely by a green and blue vehicle quickly closing the gap.

It was a hectic time, or at least until we crashed into Queens where presumably our pursuer wasn't licensed. Apart from a number of things, the district was not unlike my own. Neither had visible stars or fields of red cattle feeding luxuriously on God's good grass. I hated it. What if you were a little boy with a fishing rod, where would you go? Fishing isn't allowed in any New York cesspool known to me.

My third taxi of the night! She was a bedraggled woman of about fifteen stone. I liked her at once. She had been mistreated by her husbands—I was sure of it—and had given up on life much more precociously than most people. I resolved to give her a grandiose tip, using for that purpose the money, some of it, that I had saved from restaurants and taxicabs.

"I know so little about this district," I revealed. "Could you show me some examples of the best and worst of it?"

"Best?"

"Yes. Where there are open spaces. Red cattle in green fields and the like."

She thought.

"Well, I could take you out to Kew Gardens I suppose."

"Gardens?"

"I haven't seen them myself."

She fiddled with the radio, finding a channel to her supposed liking, and then turned westwardly and began driving at sensible speed against the grain of the December night. The decorations were testifiably fewer and further apart here, but philosophically "better-grounded," so to speak. I remarked upon a neon Santa engineered to run up and down a twenty-odd-story building with a strobe light on top. In front, I saw, I thought, two negroes kicking someone lying face-down on the pavement. It's possible of course that my prejudices had mistaken me, and these were actually Japanese. I witnessed cars beeping ferociously at each other without obvious need, a New York reflex that in my native South would have precipitated duels or fistfights even. No, my prejudices had *not* mistaken me.

"Very good," I said. "And now could you show me the *best* this area has to offer?"

She stopped and slowed, took out her compact and sought my face in the little round mirror those things hold. I didn't fail to notice the quantity of facial powder that had spilled to her lap.

"You wanted to see the worst you said, and now you want to see the best. Do I have that right?"

After a certain age, those face powders can't do much actually, as my mother had long ago confided.

"Fine woman, your mother," the driver said, picking up the thought. "Best or worst, what's it going to be?"

"Well, good gracious, I've *seen* Kew Gardens already, and so now I'd like to see what you people consider the best."

"It's two o'clock in the morning, you realize."

"Doesn't this city have any classical FM radio stations anymore? They had about twenty of them when I was young."

She dithered with the dial, settling finally upon a discussion of international trade issues. We had moved into a Slavic neighborhood peppered additionally with vibrant black youths standing motionless at five-yard intervals. The buildings here were in poor repair, and the opaque widows mirrored magnified versions of bits and pieces of the pock-marked moon. There were clues everywhere. Suddenly, that moment, something large and appreciably heavy crashed down on the hood of this woman's rather threadbare Studebaker. She increased the speed. Judging from the briny smell, I divined we were headed toward Long Island Sound; instead, she drove me up an elevation whence I could view a spacious golf course devoid, seemingly, of all forms of life.

"Alright!" I remarked. I used to hunt golf balls myself when I was a kid and sell 'em for money."

"Interesting."

"I guess I must have picked a million raspberries there, too. She'd make pies out of 'em."

"Fine woman. Ready to go back? You owe me ninety-two dollars by now."

"We used to eat those pies on the front porch. At night."

"Ninety-four now and seventy-two cents."

We left. Not wishing to delay further explorations, I directed the woman toward Manhattan, the seat of modern evil. But first, we detoured to a nearby Presbyterian Church where I hoped to relieve myself. I have always trusted in the kindness of that congregation to passersby.

The church was formal-looking and had a steeple that came to a frightful point. But first, the lady driver wanted her money and refused to take a chit. I must hand over cash money. I was owed more than two dollars in change but never got it and at my age, never tried to chase her down.

The church *was* open, but the contributions box was empty. I passed slowly down the aisle, alert to worshipers who might be sleeping in the bleachers. I had perhaps five seconds to find a toilet or otherwise my catheter wouldn't cope with the spillover. All my life, I have found the restrooms set aside for women to be better-kept, cleaner, seldom any graffiti anywhere. In this case, there were three several toilets separated by walls. I appreciated that. Micturating at leisure, I eventually lightened myself of about two pound of fluid waste and then resorted to the men's room in search of amusing inscriptions. Themselves, women have no sense of humor worth mentioning.

I had crossed a bridge, had entered Manhattan, and had urinated out of view of CCTV cameras. The contributions box was empty, but the very numerous bibles probably had some value. I ignored them and the candelabra, too. Settling into one of the forward pews, I stretched out at length and had a cigarette. There was some decent stain glass in the opposite window though my special liking was for three holy men of some sort arguing amid a flock of sheep. Or rather, one ewe in particular who brought to mind a third-grade girl I had loved at one time, her eye just as dewy as this one's.

I must have slept for a few moments, causing my cigarette to fall into the carpet's purple nap and ruin some half-square inch of it. I wasn't worried, and when I awoke and smoked, the stain glass had turned all things to red and gold.

Eight

I awoke to a Thursday morning, plodded on down to the women's facility, relieved myself, and then washed and toweled my face before I saw that I was back in my own apartment actually. I had to assume all sorts of things, namely that I had returned under my own power or someone else's. The décor was as I remembered it, even down to that star-shaped fissure in the mirror. I have always felt that my surroundings were contrivances organized by spiritual forces concerned for my welfare. I had a bed, desk, garments, and the like. There really does seem to be a special dispensation for remarkable people who deserve admiration and respect.

I ventured out into the hall and putting on a grave expression, took up next to a new recruit in a baseball cap. A more or less normal-looking individual, I offered a few comments bearing on current conditions, the weather for example, and the recent escalation in the price of platinum shares. He was a Rosicrucian militant, and I received the impression that he wanted nothing to do with me, a syndrome often found in people. Accordingly, I lifted from the chair and while maintaining the facial expression mentioned above, stepped to starboard side of our little circle, and took a place next to Lathrop thumbing through a magazine of some type.

"I told you once," said I, "that you should invest in platinum futures. But did you? Of course not."

He turned slowly and looked me in the eye. Ordinarily, I am able to withstand the gaze of the general run of people.

"Invest? I can't invest in a pair of socks."

Well, I was discombobulated by that. A prosperous person myself, reasonably prosperous, it upsets me when old men must do without socks.

"Why didn't you tell me! I could have helped you with that for Christ's sakes!"

"Not too late."

I plunged for my wallet, extracted two twenty-dollar bills, and passed the more experienced one over to him. It bore, that certificate, the portrait of a famous duelist and Indian killer, and I was loath to let it go. I advised him he should have socks all the same color lest they become mismatched in the course of events.

"I'm going to get *two* pairs," he said, "so's I can use the rest of the money for other things."

"What other things?" I started to ask.

"What other things?"

But at this point, the discussion ended. The man was depressed, and his goiter still bore the purple bruise put there by Marcus The Swine. I passed over another bill to my friend who immediately seized upon it and put it away where I couldn't see it any longer.

"No," I said, "they've got doctors today, doctors and machines that can cure all sort of diseases. Hell, they could probably get rid of that goiter altogether."

Hearing the word "goiter," he flinched and turned

his face away. His neck, too, bore a misconfiguration of some sort, the tattoo of a nude woman entwined in snakes. I didn't suppose he had ever had much to do with nude women, however. Soaked in sympathy, I passed over yet another bill, a large one this time, saying:

"They got women in this town as would canoodle with an ape, if the money is right. No! Don't ask me how I know."

He snatched the bill, read it, measured it between his thumb and forefinger and then took out a leather purse and larded it down amongst the coins. He now possessed three kinds of money secreted in three places. But even here, my compassion did not give out.

"Like a drink? I've got a bottle of Amaretto in my quarters."

That was a mistake. I detected three or four of the other boys turning to listen. Silence settled over the circle. But instead of replying, my friend simply began smacking his lips noisily, suggesting he might indeed enjoy a drink. It would be my death someday, my overload of compassion for interesting human failures. Reverting my attention to the black-and-white television set given us by one of the local charities, I witnessed a series of advertisements featuring a blue rhinoceros promoting a certain motor oil, a girl with good breasts advertising a toothpaste, George Washington, and a Chrysler car. Milbrook's dog, only he seemed immune to these inducements. Followed then a crime show centered upon a strong woman and a handsome Negro of unalloyed integrity who together had proved able week after week to identify white male weaklings and chase them down.

I pardoned myself and after summoning the dog, retreated to my quarters. I felt the same compulsive need that I had so often felt before—to separate from this

trash and resume my treks into the city, an anthropo-
logical exercise that could and should result in a book
someday. The dog was excited and refused absolutely
to obey his owner when said owner tried to hie him
back. In truth, the animal belonged more to me than to
anyone else.

Behind closed doors, I now brought together my
kit—extra socks, provender, compass, cash, and a stick
of white chalk. I loaded my .357 and checked it twice.
Could anything be more erotic than the so-called "co-
bra" ammunition that knows how to chase down a person's vital organs and turn them into waste material?
No, and now once again I promised to use *at least one
such bullet* before I died.

But hadn't trekked a whole block before Taw came
up even with me. My only and favorite friend, he pos-
sesses that rash personality, that unlikely strength, that
volcanic temper that had netted him two citizen's ar-
rests this month alone.

"You carrying?" he asked.

I hiked up my cuff to reveal the .357.

"Ammo?"

"Couple dozen rounds."

"Well alright! Let's do it then."

We proceeded forward apace. He might be under
200 pounds, but Taw is not someone you'd ever wish
unnecessarily to irritate at any time. And yet, I know
little of him, save that his mother, 92 years old now,
has lately transitioned and was badgering Taw to do
the same. His wife, by contrast, had been a darling, but
at age 32 had been burnt alive by a vibrant car driver
drunk on a new drug so recently synthesized as not to
have yet been illegalized. His father was another story.
Self-sufficient by age of nineteen, Taw had spent three
years in the service, specializing in guerilla warfare, and
even at age 74 wasn't too timid to chase bad people. He

it was who first sealed our compact with the New York Police.

"You carrying?" he asked.

His memory was not terribly good, however.

We both love the night, but this was New York City. The snow, lovely in the countryside, had turned here into a sort of brown goo that stank to heaven. Equipped with socks and leak-proof boots, we ventured where lesser men never dared intrude, even into and then out again of a tavern where the diversity coefficient bordered on illegality. Coming to a halt, we witnessed two black negroes and a Chinese-looking individual who might simply be wearing a facial tattoo. Suppressing our shared indignation, we waddled two blocks further and leapt on board a subway train offering an even more representative sample of the city's racial trash.

Across from me, I was faced with a fat woman in a short skirt. It was difficult to change seats while the train was in motion, but we succeeded in finding better scenery just twenty feet away. We must have been traveling at half-lightspeed, making it impossible to count the iron poles that theoretically supported the overhead city. I felt sick. We dashed past a uniformed man urging us forward with a lantern. The air was bad. No restroom facilities and the individual leaning up against me was snoring loudly in the world's most envied city.

I had begun to feel even iller. Two seats down, a famous lunatic was scanning the crowd through a hole in his newspaper. Normally, I am able to cause other people to look away when their eye beams challenge mine; in this case, we simply nodded, each to each. A tall woman had meanwhile gotten her neck entangled in one of the overhanging nooses. Down South, we would have rescued her immediately.

We continued to Beauregard Avenue. People who admire this species should have seen the things waiting for us on the platform. In a panic, I pushed through the crowd and with Taw just inches behind, climbed hastily to the upper world. The snowfall was adequate, making it possible to travel almost incognito, to speak so. I would have preferred a coagulated mist that forestalls people having to see each other at all. I wanted coffee and to have a smoke, but not one single café or restaurant or Christian Science Reading Room had the sort of diversity I require. In fact, I was aiming for a disregarded used bookstore—it was obvious the building was "used"— sometimes visited by me at long intervals.

This establishment really did sometimes carry good merchandise wherefore the customers were always few and far apart. Taw proceeded to the guerrilla warfare section while Milbrook's dog stayed close to me. I nodded to the antiquarian in charge and shook the snow out of my hair. An old woman was sitting on the floor rummaging among a pile of out-of-date magazines. I approached, loitered for a time, and then sat next to her.

"*Where* did you get that coffee?" I questioned. "And cigarette!"

She turned slowly and smiled. She had been beautiful in her day.

"*You* have cigarettes. Because I can see them!"

"Yes, but I'm saving them."

"Far too old to be saving things."

"Not as old as you."

"Well, I reckon not! Nobody's old as me."

I could imagine her at twenty, a pale blue evening gown, her shuddering breasts trembling independently of each other.

"What are you looking for in these old magazines? You're not going to find it of course."

"My old husband was in the service don't you see, and I'm just sure there's a photograph of him somewhere."

"You must have other photos of him for Christ's sakes."

"I did. But we had that fire."

"Wait a minute. You lost your husband in the war and now you don't have any photos of him? My God, that may be the most pathetic thing I ever heard.

What did he look like? If you can remember."

"Well, he was tall. Pretty tall."

I gathered some twenty or thirty copies of the journal and began splashing through them, but then finding nothing, wandered on down to the historical section where alone in post-modern times decent prose may still be found. I care not at all, as I've said before, for accuracy in these accounts, no more than I care for the price of the items in my coin and stamp collections. In these matters, I care but for beauty and that only. For not only are beauty and virtue the very same thing, beauty is better.

I found myself confronted then with a full range of used and tattered copies of quaint and curious volumes, as Poe described it, of historical lore. I alit upon MacIntosh's 1704 account of events deemed important by him for the period under consideration. The covers were a bit fatigued to be sure and harkened back to the period to be described further down. A worthless report and long ago superseded, I returned the book to its three-inch niche between a leather-bound example of the 1909 *Finding the North Pole* with an introduction by Admiral Melville. It pleased me that the storeowner offered his wares in such random sequence, as if he understood the actual nature of time and its contortions. The best of this particular book was shown in the gravures between pages 184 and 185 where a grampus (?)

was seen attacking a narwhal (?). The next book was of course an exposition of Jefferson's thought and actions produced by an Assistant Professor in search of tenure. I had already read perhaps 20% of these titles, leaving me with not very much headspace for more. I perceived then that notorious monograph on Nazi-Soviet relations, a cunning exposition by a world-famous Leninist. Standing on tiptoes, I was able to relocate the vile thing to a place where it would not likely be seen again.

Thus passed the time until at 1:16 when I collided into a little old man furrowing through the Greek, Roman, and Byzantine shelves. I do take *some* care with my personal presentation whereas this person took none.

"Egad," said I. "Some pretty good stuff here."

"Indeed."

"You'll be a professor," I ventured. "Retired. A retired classics professor, am I right?"

"Not really, no. No, I'm more the freelance type."

"Retired freelance classics professor."

"No, I were never a professor."

His voice was reedy and seemed to come from far away. He was dressed in the very best kind of clothes, now largely in decay. He had a vitelline stain on a cutoff tie about six inches too short. And, too, the lenses in his wire glasses had been ground to very different prescriptions, lending him a look of great astuteness. The nose was bad and resembled a potato. His cufflinks imitated Roman coins and maybe were. A stalwart man, he wore sandals in lieu of shoes and did without socks. I liked him at once.

"Alcman had a funny nose," I offered, "but everyone admired him anyway."

"Alcman! I've done some work on that fellow."

"Published?"

"Hardly. Who would publish *me*?"

"Ah. I see what you mean."

We sat. His teeth were few, and he spoke with a lisp. His watchband was of real or imitation gold, and gold, too, was the encrusted container kept in his vest to hold a choice of cigarettes. I chose a long skinny one bent in the middle.

"You don't want *that*," he said taking it back. "Take this."

It was short and fat, this one, and I had trouble putting it alight. I turned my attention to the three several used books the man had chosen, one of them also short and fat and the others much less so. He had chosen well. I espied volume II of Klyuchevsky's *History* stressed by the great number of ill-chosen bookmarks torn from newspapers and other sources. And so here then was an authentic scholar, quite unlike my hallmates back at the Midas Hotel.

"Fine stuff, fine stuff I say," said I, referring to these materials. "But I took you for a classicist plain and simple."

"Not really, no. No, I just happen to have fixed on that area between the Elbe and the Dnieper."

"Understandable."

"Where bad things were most likely to happen."

"Indeed. Of course, we have some bad things here, too."

We laughed, both, and then served ourselves to another cup of coffee.

"I have a Sophocles incunabulum," I said suddenly, the first time in weeks I had admitted that to anyone.

He jumped back.

"Liar."

"No, really! Aldine. 1498."

"I'll have to assay that, if I'm to believe it."

I helped him gather up his books and while holding the Klyuchevsky (heavy!) in my arms, stood by while he

traipsed up to the strange owner and paid for his pur-
chases out of his pouch. I descried a thousand-dollar
green bill among the lesser currencies. And yet, to
come to this place, he had had to travel through an African settlement with aborigines posted at every corner.
Clearly, he was as educated as me and unless he had a
gun, considerably braver.

I was pleased when the proprietor wrapped each
book separately in a fine rice paper and sealed them
with a mucilage of some kind. I don't know how much
my friend had to pay for this merchandise, but I'm wa-
gering it was no piffling amount. Once outside, we
trekked for two blocks before remembering to come
back for Taw and pay for the Klyuchevsky. It was by
now almost three in the morning, and the goddamned
New York Times was already decanting bundles of the
Morning Edition onto street corners where black derelicts were waiting to poison passers-by with printed
lies. A transgressive action, we three lit up cigarettes in
plain open view and expelled the smoke from our half-
dozen nostrils.

We strode past a sex shop but then came back to
check the artifacts on display. There were of course the
usual sex drones, one of them more than eight feet tall
and another a perfect simulacrum of a nine-year-old
child with an angelic face. The male drones, most of
them, were incarnations of famous movie stars and rap
musicians. We tried to analyze some of the implements
on offer though they proved too complicated for us old
people correctly to interpret.

It began to rain, my favorite weather. The classicist,
by contrast, loathed it. Hunched over his books, he
went forward a few paces and of a sudden ducked into
a restaurant of some sort where four or five journalists—they looked like journalists—were seated at the
bar. Much fatter than they should have been, they

touched each other at buttock and belly both. I wanted to leave; instead, Taw pulled me in after him and directed us to a remote table hardly visible at such a distance. He glared severely at the youths gathered there till finally they gathered their mugs and went away. The old man's books had *not* been harmed by the rain, or not at first sighting anyway. Did he intend to inspect each and every page?

The waitresses, both, were plain-enough-looking but dressed in berets. Inspired by that, the scholar ordered a "croissant," for Christ's sakes, while Taw and I ordered alcoholic drinks. The ambiance here was good, I admit it, and there are worse things in this world than lurking in a dark corner with refined persons while laughing at New Yorkers running past in an opaque rain. It was 4:17 in the morning, remember. I saw a woman in seven-inch heels stumble and fall and had to fight my Southern heritage to keep from going to help her. The scholar had meantime thumbed his way through perhaps 12% of his Klyuchevsky and thus far had found no damage nor anything else to impair the text. He began reading out loud. Knowing nothing of that bizarre language, I turned away and focused on my drink. Bored past endurance, Taw was continually tapping two fingers and sometimes a third and then standing and sitting again. He wore a blue sweater and from a distance would have seemed no older than seventy-two or three. After five minutes of this, I took out my bookstore receipt and for the sake of future readers began jotting down notes about my friends and their behavior.

We left that place in good time and then rambled down Antonescu Avenue for perhaps a quarter-mile, halting only when Taw descried a medium-size African taking money from passersby. Were it cocaine he was offering, or meth perhaps, or LSD, or horse medicine, or cigarettes, or mayhap one of the newer compounds? We consulted, we three, asking whether we should or even could punish this individual in proper fashion. It was Taw, of course, who actually did stroll to the "person" and then took out some money and showed it. A significant conversation ensued. Of all common medicaments, only aloe held any appeal for Taw. We watched and waited, the nervous classicist, Milbrook's dog, and I. My .357 was loaded and yearning to be used, but I wasn't prepared to unleash the thing as long as some dozen potential witnesses were milling about within view of the scene.

As always, some moments passed. Too cautious and too old to snap the blighter's neck with his own strength alone, my favorite friend had cajoled the tradesman toward and then into the narrow dark space separating the two buildings that staged the scene, a better place, he must have supposed, for doing business. It needed not long for us to join them. Possibly you've seen a negro's eyes when their owner feels endangered? Two wads of cotton affixed to a 1950s grammar-school blackboard. We restrained the dog.

"What are you offering?" I politely asked the by-now-terrified jigaboo. "Heroin? Or cocaine?"

"No, man, I don't do that shit no mo! I don't lie about shit like that! My mama daddy be an old white guy like you!"

"So, what *do* you sell?"

"Nothing! Okay, I won't lie. I has to, like, take care my babies, you feel me, and so's I deal some of that new stuff. Know what I'm talking about?"

"Yes. Okay, take off your clothes."

"Say what? Sheeet! You dudes is craaazy!"

We edged closer. Very calmly, I hoisted my trouser leg to reveal my ankle holster and its content. He looked at it. He seemed to believe we craved his black ass, but after we had reasoned with him, he did at last divest himself of his overcoat, jeans, and panties. Seeing that prehistoric body in moonlight, I came near to vomiting.

"Good! Now we want you to run down this alley and come out the other side, and then we want you to run around town for a couple of hours. Don't call for help, okay, largely because I have your phone. Feel me? We'll be watching every step of the way, know what I'm talking about?"

"I got my rights!"

"What you got," Taw exposed, "is Vade's Smith and Wesson about an inch deep in your right kidney."

He examined, first, the hand with the Smith and Wesson and soon after the gun itself. I had not expected the scholar to be the first to burst out laughing, owing perhaps to the negro's inept running style.

We gathered the white pills left behind and offered them free of charge to the random negroes passing by. They appeared suspicious at first, one of them actually declining the benefit. By now, it was a good deal later than had earlier been the case and we still had some distance between ourselves and safe harbor.

It was even later when at last we came to the containment to find the men with but few exceptions sleeping in the hall. We went from face to face and speaking softly, gave judgements on the character of each person.

"Oh my gosh," said my friend. "Lucien writes about people like this. Look at that one."

He was right. It was an open and shut case of a Jew plain and simple, his dead eyes studying back at us through translucent lids. The stench was horrendous, and at my age my sense of balance was already problematic. We retreated quick into my apartment but not even there could we shelter against the snoring and groaning of old men suffering from the memory of their sins.

Locked away in my apartment, I excused myself long enough to complete a long-form police report on our actions. I could safely expect a good payment for this. Next, I opened my cabinet and exposed my beer can collection to my visitors. The classicist, conscious of the short number of licensed breweries outside of Bucharest itself, dove into the stuff, rummaging excitedly among my Romanian material. I had experienced considerable difficulty ensuring these collectibles, having finally to resort to a low-cost broker found loitering outside a bodega up on 53rd Street. Meantime, I kept close watch on my friend. He was quick with his hands and prone to drooling and at the end of day, or night rather, had proved incapable of tasting nighttime New York City to its lees. As to Taw, never a great lover of beers, he quickly grew bored with it and after wishing us a pleasant night, or day rather, gathered himself up and repaired to his own apartment.

We shared, the scholar and I, a couple of psychotropics needed by people of our kind. My friend had a tic in his left eyelid, and he tended to stutter when he came to conversational topics. His eyes, too, were a problem, the result, one must suppose, of his granulated retinas.

Outside, a false dawn had made a brief appearance on the other side of my window, allowing us the quick view of an undressed negro racing down the avenue. But now, it was real dark out there again. My guest arose, shook the cigarette ashes from his lap, and bid me farewell in cordial style. I let him go. His Greek was no doubt better than mine while I had no Russian at all, but when it comes to racial loathing, that boy's not even an amateur.

Forcing a pathway through the dreaming thralls, I

escorted him to the door. Another minute and my hallmates would be awakening and singing roundelays of uninterrupted complaint. I was congratulating myself for having come away with volume three of the Kluychevsky, and it wasn't till I had returned to my own room that I conceded that I had lost my wallet. Classicist indeed, he had proved a plain simple thief.

Nine

Late as it was, I *was* able to get back down into the city before my fellow residents came fully awake. The incidents of the following hours were interesting, fairly interesting, but now I want to skip ahead to March 4th when I accrued a full nine hours of garden-variety sleep with but two interludes to be described, time permitting, later on.

A clear night, that of March 4th, and after taking two lines of medicine, I was eager to put myself back into the milieu once more. At the first intersection, I encountered a man who bore an uncanny resemblance to Edvard Munch's most famous portrayal, but then moved past him without speaking. It isn't always easy to separate the new-style sex drones from our more traditional whores, save that the drones are equipped with narrow slots in their foreheads for credit cards. I moved past one such creature, a "Clark Gable" robot designed, I supposed, for octogenarian girls. You remember when Paris offered those street-side pissoirs where citizens could void their bladders with their faces exposed to public view? As an aside, let me say that I possess a picture album, a picture album I say, of some 23 such faces.

Halfway down Horthy Street, I slipped into a novelty shop doing a brisk business at just past five in the morning. To be sure, the shop, or niche rather was

congested with smiling youths pawing the artificial ex-
crement, the bunny ears, etc., while for my part I was
more interested in the good variety of polyurethane
masks on offer. I donned one such product simulating
Harry S. Truman and went to the mirror. But that man
was never as heavy as me, and I exchanged it for the
official 1941 Julius Streicher. Now that individual really
was as focused as I am wont to be, and if slightly shorter, his gait and personal jollity corresponded significantly with my own. I paid for the thing out of my own
money and asked for the cashier's assistance in putting
it on. There *was* a changing room, a mere closet really,
but also furnished with a pee-pot that had presented
itself just in the nick of time. The mask was a bit too
small but with the aid of scissors, the clerk was able to
make place for my nose. Highly satisfied, I exited the
place, traveled two blocks, and then diverged into a
street never seen before either by me nor very many
others.

I often find that I become so unaware of my masks
that I will sometimes try to superimpose another. But
not tonight. Tonight was for other things even if I
could not right away say what those things were. I
moved slowly past the famous *Heartbreak Hotel*, forcing my way through a crowd of miniature bellhops all
dressed in black. My immediate need was for a glass of
something or another, a good old black-and-white
movie, an Egyptian cigarette, or to turn about right
now and go back to the hostel; instead, I did none of
those but on the contrary continued on until in the
consummation of time I and the man following me
blundered onto a video place full of rotten youths ec-
staticizing noisily among a great many very evil-looking
machines. I joined them, migrating instinctively to a
neon-lit apparatus as large almost as a car or car and a
half with images of naked ladies running across the

screen. For a dollar, a player could shoot electronic darts at these people causing realistic wounds of all sorts. I might have joined myself, but that I wasn't willing (yet) to take out my wallet and permit my money to be seen. There were some Jews in the place, not to mention representatives of some of the major west African tribes. Of women, there were few, and even these were not indisputably female. One of them, a "woman" of perhaps fifty, had the tattoo of an octopus on her décolletage but also seemed to recognize the likeness covering my own face. I felt a hand in my back pocket and swirled around to see the person as had been following me, smiling back agreeably. Because I'm from Alabama, they think me fool enough to carry my money *there*? I had no option but to go into my vest and flaunt the actual money to his face.

Returned to the street, I found that I needed to piss, or anyway wanted to. Accordingly, I dodged into a variety shop and barged into the facility where a fat man was sitting on the toilet. Too stubborn to move, he simply went into a hypnogogic state while pretending inauthentically to snore. I had no alternative but to use the sink clogged already with paper towels and cigarette butts in the world's most enviable city.

The shop itself did offer a variety of things. I examined a programmable kinetic robot able to do all manner of things. The price, alas, was out of reach. I chatted with a little old lady who, to be truthful, was not probably as old as me. She told of another outlet over in Queens where for a trivial fee, drunks and other derelicts could be viewed fighting with baseball bats in the back room. We exchanged cigarettes, but then exchanged back again once we sampled what we had received. I toyed with a toy rifle, and then tried out a ballpoint pen that ejected ink into the user's face. Amused, I drifted to the "pharmaceutical" counter but dared not, believe me, invest in the stuff. A mechanical dog had come up to gnaw upon my cuff, but then immediately left off when she sighted Milbrook's dog.

It was already early morning, and I still had much to do. I turned in at the next police headquarters and while behaving with extreme courtesy, devoted a few minutes to downloading some of the clues I had witnessed up and down Sunflower Street. From overhead, someone suddenly screamed out in hideous pain. I urinated. A not unkindly man, the officer had taken out his handkerchief and was proffering it to me. In reply, I offered him a gratuity, which he declined, and then exited by the side door in hopes of foiling the person following me all night long.

Nothing ever ceases in this macabre city, and I am no longer surprised to come upon hardware stores, pharmacies, and even mortuaries open for business all around the clock. Make money, lots and quickly, or die a hideous death in New York City! I then stumbled upon a bookshop of some kind, a narrow opening between chalk-colored storefronts that extended up and down the road. Here, the stain glass window was chalk-colored also and portrayed a Sassanian knight impaling an unlucky Christian on his lengthy lance. Bringing Milbrook's dog with me—at this hour he looked like a puff of cotton candy suspended about three inches above the pavement in the granular light—we made haste to get inside that place before too late.

Two clerks, females both, the short one dressed in clothes and the other a licorice stick about six feet and one or two inches tall. Because I don't talk about books with negroes, I applied to the more abbreviated one. Her pupils, clear as water, went on changing shape as I drew near. I could see at least some hint of her genetic code in those inconstant orbs.

"Hello, I say" said I, "French and German mostly I

say. Also, a bit of Scotch-Irish perhaps?"

"Italian," she said. "And some Romanian, but I don't know how much."

"Romanian! I knew it! Fucking Romanians! I think I'm in love with you!" And then, after a moment's thought: "But of course, we don't know what Romanians really are, do we?"

"No, sir."

"All those centuries after the Romans left. You may be half-gypsy for all I know. Or Scythian even."

She looked down. Her nose was exceptionally adorable, however, and that melted me.

"No, no, that's alright, perfectly alright. What was Codreanu's ancestry after all? We just don't know."

She looked up.

"My great-grandfather."

I was floored by that, needless to say, and required half a minute to get back up again. Her nose and forehead and upper arms were better than I had understood, wherefore I pulled her aside to discuss for the next quarter-hour her provenance and other things. That span of time having come and gone, I said:

"Last week, I read A. H. Foib's new novel, his best, I think. But I thought that fellow was dead!"

"Yes, sir. He died in '17."

"I see. Well how the devil is he still writing books then?"

"Gosh. I don't know. Maybe we could ask his publisher?"

The publisher was over on ---------- Street, a sprightly distance from my then location. Nor was the morning growing any younger. I thanked the lady graciously, handed her a twenty, and then went back outside where for the nonce it wasn't actually snowing.

I traveled far on that night, comparatively far, and was required two times to stop and piss. My personal compass was broken, or perhaps the city's polarity was askew again; in any case, the pastel buildings and people continued on endlessly as it seemed, even to the Gulf of Mexico, to speak in that exaggerated fashion. I saw a man without legs moving sideways at high speed, but then slapped myself on the forehead to be reminded that in fact I was still intoxicated on medicine. I drew my gun, which seemed to soften in my hand, the opening pointing down at the ground, etc.

I passed many people prior to the following hour, yes, and buildings, too. I confronted a black jigaboo with a tin cup playing an accordion. Approaching fearlessly, I asked for a romantic ballad from my own decade. He kept his eye upon mine, proving beyond doubt that not only was he *not* blind, but instead the other way around. As for the cup, someone had spat in it, soaking the single one-dollar piece of paper currency it contained. Alright, there might have been a few coins as well. One block further, I made a 90-degree turn and darted into a dark alley to urinate. I had had a half-quart of buttermilk during the foregoing day and must now be releasing it at brief intervals.

Thereafter, I came to yet another franchise bookstore served by yet another thirty-year-old well-dressed ivy-league female progressive levitating in a cloud of hauteur. But rather than setting foot in the place, I merely pulled open the door and called to her in a gender-neutral voice. In fact, I was asking about the publisher of Foib's new book. She did answer, but her northern accent was simply too much for my poor ears.

I plodded on, my septuagenarian quiddities in full open view. That was the moment it reoccurred to me that somewhere along the way, an old-fashioned telephone directory might be housed. I turned and went back to that notable drugstore noted before, a place so out-of-phase with modernity that milkshakes and vanilla sodas even now were available. I asked for a double portion of ice cream, and as I sat ogling the girl three seats down, I inquired insouciantly as to whether the place hosted a telephone directory. She made a face, the girl behind the counter, exposing a dime-size location just between the eyebrows where a .357 artillery shell could have painted the whole establishment a bright brilliant red. But in that case, she wouldn't actually have felt anything. The brain, it is said, is as immune to pain as a piece of cauliflower of the same size.

The directory was thick, thicker than the printed menu though not as thick as my own very partial copy of the *Monumenta Germaniae Historica*. In casual mode, I splashed through the pages till I hit upon the sought publishing company now domiciled at 153–157 Third Avenue in New York City. Right away, I began to look for a taxicab, but then soon came back to exit the place and pay for my soda. Cabs hesitate to take me on board, and the pilots, if they merit that name, come usually from the lower strata of New York capitalism. My own driver, a dubious type, didn't reply to that comment. In truth, he turned out to be a Turkic sort of being who confessed finally that his wives were still in Kirgizstan but would be rejoining him soon. He did drive well, goddamn him, and before I could finish one of my long thin Egyptian cigarettes, we had crossed a good part of the East River entrained just then with slowly-moving coal barges guided by strobe lights. I had managed to free myself (I thought) of the cretin who had been following me for the last seven hours, and now began to prepare myself to set foot once again on world-famous Manhattan Island.

I left the car and strode for perhaps fifty yards before the driver came up even with me and began yelling for his payment. Having never wanted to cheat the fellow, I also gave him a cigarette. Or rather a blunt, if you feel me. In front, I discovered a huge advertisement showing a beautiful anfractuous girl in a bathing suit. The city was so odd at this hour, as if a beneficent plague had taken all but the essential people. Came then a lorry dispensing copies of the excrementitious *New York Times*. I did manage to dodge the bundle thrown in my direction and proceeded on to Knickerbocker Avenue where I paused to view the faces in the windows of the above-ground subway loitering at the platform. A woman, seemingly normal, had fallen to sleep in the upright position. Coming nearer, I scrutinized her closely, finding evidence of unconfessed tragedies in her lorn aspect. A veritable palimpsest, that face, with evidences of integrity still to be seen in the second layer. How many, pray, how many loutish males I ask had used her up and thrown her away? I may be an annoyingly altruistic sort of individual, but no one can indict my partiality for women, the world's martyrs fallen to earth to offer love to the sort of wretches visible in other parts of that subway car!

I proceeded deeper into the urban pustule, all times aware that I might soon need to piss. I moved past an infamous Rastafarian monastery and after checking behind me, hurried to the other side of the road where I discerned a small yellow drone with two nozzles hovering just overhead. The previous night's rain had been a disappointment to be supplanted by what now promised to be an eight-on-a-ten-scale snowfall. Never is this city less hideous than when three-fourths hidden under snow. A planetary traveler might even consider halting here for a cup of coffee. I moved past an octoroon reticulated with tattoos resembling spider webs. Could anything be more out-of-phase than negros and snow? I don't think so, wherefore I edged into a coffee shop predestined ten million years ago for my convenience alone.

There was a person behind the counter, feasibly a woman who had long ago given up on life and had simply been waiting all this time for me to come along.

"G'morning!" I said jauntily in my way. "Here I am!"

She smiled, her friendliness quickly draining away as she took a better view either of me or perhaps someone hiding behind me. I took a better view of her, too. No doubt her breasts had at one time been accoutrements offering delight to male eyes, but not now, now that she had lost interest in them and no longer bothered to position them to advantage. On the other hand, the smell of coffee invested the place, and there was a touristic photo of the Empire State Building just behind the cash register. The lady quickly served me with a cup of putative good coffee and now was sweetening it to her own prescription.

"Really coming down out there!" said I in referring to what was coming down out there.

"Better out there than in here."

"Indeed."

I lifted my cup and toasted her, but then soon had to return the cup to its saucer when I saw how hot it was.

"You seem to be all alone here tonight," I mooted.

She jumped back. There might or might not have been a gun of some kind behind the counter. Hoping to allay her, I took out my cigarette case and offered her a bunt which she accepted shyly. There was no breeze inside the diner, but she cupped her worn-out hands around the match anyhow. I thought I could read some of her experiences in the injuries to that hand. Her hide was freckled and half-transparent, and I could make out the bones, some of them, and the integuments that manipulated. She'd be dead within a decade, I suggested, and the protoplasmic armor that will have shielded her up until that time will have become unrecognizable to family, friends, and old-time lovers alike.

"I bet you got all kinds of money in that there cash register," I mooted, standing suddenly and transferring myself to a better position. In the meantime, one of the pedestrians had come to the window and was pressing at the glass. I was disinclined to allow him inside even if his face and overall demeanor wasn't as bad as it so easily might have been.

The woman conjectured: "He wants to come inside and have a cup of coffee I suppose."

"Can't. His nose has frozen to the glass."

She laughed, or tried to, and then threw up her hand and beckoned the son-of-a-bitch to come inside. He was roseate and plump, and I reasoned that the orangutan who had birthed him probably had those same issues as well. Although too small by much, he did seem an adult. We watched amusedly as he entered, faded to the toilet, shut the door, flushed, and then came out and linked up with the pinball machine. We laughed and by the time he took a place as far from me as possible, the proprietress had already poured and sweetened (very lightly) his cup of coffee.

"Really coming down out there," he exposed in his northeastern voice.

"Better out there than in here."

He agreed in general terms. Although not actually a Jew or negro, his head had that anti-white shape and lamentable moustache that suggested he had lived in this town for very long.

"It's not just snow nor even rain," I said politely, "but rising sea levels that put us in such great peril. Pretty soon, we'll all have to move to, like, Alabama."

"Rather be dead."

"Yes, for you, I'd prefer that, too."

He stood, not that he had ever truly sat. We had disliked each other since before we were born, and now we were reacting like those early sapiens when first they discovered Neanderthals pestering their women. He was of course much younger than me but also smaller. A man like that with a face like his was almost certainly unarmed.

"Not very nice, to say a thing like that."

"How much do you weigh actually?"

We circled, taking care not to slip and fall in the molted snow the rectum had brought with him. As ancient as I am and as slow, I'd have to accept two or three blows before effectively coming to grips with this New Yorker.

"Alright," said I, always speaking politely, "I might have to take even four or five blows, but we both know what the end will be."

"Possibly."

"One blow, just one blow from my ham-fisted fist and . . ."

"I see. And yet, all I ever wanted was just a cup of coffee."

I nodded to the woman to give the "man" what he wanted. I knew from experience, or from observation anyway, that the best moment for launching an attack is when the enemy is trying to gulp down a cup of hot coffee.

Day was dawning in the usual East when I came outside and, dismayed by the filthy sun bouncing off the cars and getting into peoples' eyes, trudged forward for perhaps two hundred rods before getting back into my mask.

I was tired, tired not only of my own life but even more so that of others. My mask was in place and my headset, too, but I couldn't pick up with the Arensky concerto against the sound of traffic running in the slush. The women, perhaps fifteen percent of them, were in high heels that left coin-size "fingerprints" (shoe prints actually) in the two-inch snowfall. Let me pitch forward face-first onto the walkway and those shoes would very quickly have punctured me to death. I opted therefore to beckon a cab and jump inside it.

I still sometimes dream of hailing a taxi that doesn't already have other passengers, in this case a Near- or Middle-Eastern sort of individual with a woven beard. I don't myself bathe very often, but this woman had surpassed me by weeks. I smiled, offered her a stub, and then got into my sunglasses on account of the rays and sunbeams. She refused my offer. I no longer carry snuff. She looked to me rather like a jihadist or dervish, but I remained quiet throughout. We were traveling through some of the priciest purlieus of Manhattan, a domain without soil or cattle or space enough for a petunia bed. I pined for the piney woods of reasonable Alabama. Turned I then to the Muslim, whispering:

"I have no intention of converting, none. So, what are you going to do about that?"

She did actually reply, but her voice had so much of that sinuous quality of Arabic script that I couldn't even make aught of it.

"A pederast, of course, your prophet."

We coasted the length of the Avenue of the Americas and then diverged into a pixelated neighborhood populated by a characteristic sort of people. I had wanted to be taken, and was, to one of the bridges leading to Manhattan where I departed the taxi. In the distance, I could hear the digestive noise of millions of computers sorting out the news. Trying to earn a living, these people! I have read infinite pages of Herodotus and Sima Qian without once having to be reminded of how *those* people earned a living. They just didn't care about such trivia. I still needed to piss but had first to walk back an appreciable distance to pay the driver.

My jacket was lined with fleece, and I was indifferent to the wind. If I can stand up to temperatures of 104 in Alabama, 6 degrees in New York is beneath contempt. The snow was lovely—I admit it—and looked like a flight of moths colluding in midair. The cold was unrelenting and never mind the sheepskin jacket purportedly protecting my withered torso. I yearned for doughnuts and coffee; instead, I extracted my third-to-last standard cigarette and attempted all quite in vain to ignite it on the bridge. If I wanted to urinate from this position, the stuff would blow back into my face; accordingly, I resorted to the intubation strapped to my right leg and permitted the "tear drops" to leave a little trail to aid the slackers moving up behind.

Manhattan is wonderful in the morning—you believe that?—and the Jews were chomping at the bit to get down to the futures exchange. My diseased mind turned to the sea life down below and the look of snowflakes drifting on the stream. But how did I happen to be in such a predicament at this precise juncture in the time-space continuum? I promise to tell all about it later on.

All my life, I have wanted to spend fulltime catering to my genius; instead, I now found myself squinting into the raw ionized sunlight assailing the entire apparent length of --------- Avenue. It was a long distance between this place and others, never mind between the others themselves, and I was not willing, indeed not probably capable of strolling so far under my own authority. Even so, I did wish to sample the district and its cultural disposition at this early moment with its many office workers scattering hastily to their consignments. I doubt even the Spartans mustering before Plataea were in such a hurry. And these anxious faces! Your ordinary twelfth-century yeoman never suffered like that. And yet, this was the most besought address in the whole post-modern former West. I do hope there will be a good civilization someday, but I shan't be alive to see how it reckons with the twenty-first-century United States.

I wasn't sure I could walk any further. I did perceive one place where elderly men might urinate, but I didn't much care for the looks of those waiting in line. In Lacedemonia, there was hardly any place where a man couldn't urinate and women, too. Nevertheless, I continued on for perhaps a thousand rods, passing in the shadow of insurance companies, health clubs, brokerages, and other tall buildings containing God knows what. I passed a department store displaying tons of superfluous materials never seen before. Very hurriedly, I sprinted inside and loped to the facility where only one sole male had arrived before me. I nodded to him, but he nodded not to me. The graffiti was decent, fairly decent, including a watercolor that would have ecstaticized a psychiatrist. In the clothing section, I was encouraged to find that mannikins had at last begun to give she-males their percentage.

Outside and on both sides of the street, the snow was paving over the earlier layers with a new and more crystalline material that looked a bit like Gulf Coast sand. One almost expected to see little white crabs scampering hither and yon (not really) and gulls drifting overhead. I made haste to cross to that side but then turned and worked my way back through the traffic. From this new, or rather previous angle, I had a far better view of the upper stories of the gigantic hotel across the way. I could see people up there and envied them for their warmth and privileged point of view, but especially the little boy on the ninth floor drawing pictures in the window frost.

I moved westward for perhaps an eighth-mile and then continued in that direction for four blocks further.

It has always been my policy to look upon the world as if it had never been seen before by me or even others. The people, adorned in fabric clothes, wanted to protect themselves from the weather, a financial expense that made them more awkward than need be. Somewhere on another moon or planet, such inconveniences have never arisen in the first place—such was just one of the reasons for my bitterness at having come to life at this particular time and place. I knew where I was going and knew where it was, and knew I would stop when I got there, the typical attitude for people going places. In a better world, superior people who feast out of their own intellectual pantries need never go anywhere at all.

I did in the fullness of time come to the headquarters of that famous publishing concern that had emitted the new novel said to have been written by my favorite writer. The lobby was warm but the receptionist cold, and the wall offered portraits of female "authors" only. I stepped forward, hiding my cigarette behind my back. She had, the receptionist, the beginnings of a moustache, a venal sin on the part of women who might otherwise have been almost attractive. What kind of husband would allow that? Her blouse was no good either and tended to obviate the expected appurtenances.

"A good man, your husband. But can you point me to the editor of this novel?" I asked, giving her the imprint information.

She looked at me.

"The editor," I reiterated.

"You wish to speak to one of our editors?"

"I do. The editor of the novel above described."

"We have lots of editors."

"Good."

"But you don't imagine they spend a lot of time here

in this building, do you?"

(Actually, I did.)

"Alright, so let me speak to some *other* editor then, a white one and old."

She groaned. Her hair was short, and she had no husband, of that I was by now assured. Her fingernails had faces on them, multicultural ones. Had only I a pair of plyers, I could easily have removed her nails and moustache both.

In the event, I was seconded to the elevator and thence to the third floor where a certain Mr. Saunders maintained a one-person office. His hair was braided, and he bore the tattoo on his neck of a magical symbol. This man could have crumpled me effortlessly into a ball and dropped me to the sidewalk, his arms were that large.

"So, what's *your* problem?" he asked, coming to a stance.

"Didn't get much sleep."

"What?"

"No, actually I just wanted to speak with a certain editor. Or any editor. If I knew where he lives. Or she."

"Oh boy, another one. I've got a job to do, and here they come. You don't got a phone directory?"

"Yes, but I don't know these peoples' names actually."

"Names? They're in the directory for Christ's sakes!"

I apologized, dropped my cigarette to the carpet, and backed from the room. I believed that I could hear the printing press rumbling from one of the upper stories, a gigantic machine, as I conceived it, running over with pulp of all sorts. I proceeded slowly down the hall, peering discretely into the cells on both sides. I espied a bespectacled woman of some kind speaking rapidly into a machine that was speaking back. Devoid of any sort of sexual value, her hair, I admit, *was* a grade or two above the normal standard. As said before, I have chosen to look upon civilization the way protozoa do, as if viewing it for the first time. She wore hose, had earrings, and there was a calendar on the wall.

"Yes?" she said, removing her glasses. "Can I help?"

I drew my own glasses and got into them. At once, I noted that inevitable flabbiness that afflicts the upper arms of women past the age of, say, 27.

"I'm looking for an editor," I said. "And any of them will do."

"Have you tried Mr. Saunders' office?"

"In a word, yes."

"And was he able to help?"

"Probably."

She laughed. Not entirely a bad person, she, too, had no doubt had dealings with that person.

"Perhaps you should use the phone directory."

"I don't know their names."

"They're in there. Except maybe not Lloyd's."

"Lloyd! And where does *he* live?'

"Amalfi coast, last I heard."

She had repositioned her glasses and was threatening to go back to work. I could feel my gorge rising.

"I think maybe *you're* an editor, hmm?"

But she continued speaking into that machine of hers. Awkward most times, I stepped more or less adeptly into her chamber and set about examining the some 50 or 60 books disarranged in her insignificant bookcase. Some of these titles, most of them probably, had been issued by this very self-same company. I have already explained how in my opinion books ought to be organized. Meanwhile, her neck had become vulnerable to an icepick attack, though I wasn't yet ready for that.

"I think you may be doing a patch of editing *right now*, even as you and I sit and stand here. Am I right?"

She turned and scrutinized Streicher's face. Slowly and slowly, she was becoming amused by me, fascinated even, and seriously alarmed. Her voice when she spoke was just as it had been when first I heard it.

"I was *trying* to finish something. Before you interrupted. And I don't even know who you are!"

"We do need good editors in this country. People like you." (I offered her a blunt.) "Are you perchance she who edited Foib's new novel? He's dead, don't you know."

Her interest increased. All my life, I've been able to get inside people's heads and bother them a great deal.

"Are *you* Foib?" she asked in seeming earnest.

"Me? Hardly. That ole boy had rather be dead than visit New York."

She now laughed out loud, a negative action with regard to the crow's feet about her lips and teeth. And yet, she was not a bad egg for this region, and I was encouraged by her overall person to invite her to join me for a drink.

I dislike walking next to a woman who is only slightly shorter than myself and therefore made an effort to move on tiptoes. Except for me and she and a vending machine, the hall was largely empty, and our footfalls could no doubt be heard for a short distance. She was still amused—good—but I knew it wouldn't last for long. She wore a wedding band on the appropriate finger, but it looked to me more like a placebo. She was almost pretty in the shrouded light, but I did not at this time gather her in my atrophied hands and kiss her on her tangerine lips, a task I leave to others.

There were three other persons waiting in the elevator, each of them facing off in the direction of his or her own choosing. My companion was still sexually active, I divined, though the periodicity was of course spreading out. I was surprised when one of the other passengers turned suddenly and let his face be seen. I knew that we would soon be leaving the elevator and soon thereafter edging out into the street. On the other hand, an experienced person can never be absolutely sure of anything.

We did, as foretold, move out into the madding street. It was nearly noon at this time and the lunchtime thralls were skittering back and forth in search of vitalization. Or rather, in search of a half-hour's separation from their fellow bees. We marched resolutely in an eastern direction toward a purported coffee shop. We stepped inside and glanced about and after ascertaining that the diversity ratio was acceptable, stepped hastily to a small round table associated with three small chairs and settled ourselves before others could claim the place. She was still amused, my date, and already was logging this as one of her best adventures in years.

"Good! And so, here we are after all. In truth, it does smell like coffee in here. Now tell me where Lloyd is staying these days."

"Hm? Vacationing in Italy I believe."

"I doubt it. No, just tell me the street at least."

"I don't have to tell you anything."

Less amused than herebefore, she made as if to arise. To allay that, I positioned my much heavier foot on top her wee one.

"You want I should grind your toes to dust? Break off your five-inch heels? Ram both of them into your equal number of ears? *Where does he live*, that malefactor, or else you can expect . . . Do I need tell you what you can expect?"

"No. No sir, I mean. I'm feeling queasy just now. How do you do that?"

I had not half finished my coffee and in fact had determined not to finish it at all. Not that it wasn't a decent brew, but just that I had elected not to go on with it any further.

"And you, too? Not going to finish your coffee?"

"I'm too nervous."

"As well you should be! Alright, we'll just wait here till you've settled down a little bit. That will give you time to hand over your goddamn little digital phone so's you won't be making use of it behind my back."

"'So's'? Who talks like that anymore? Besides, I need to go to the ladies' room."

"'Ladies'? In New York?"

She tried to laugh and actually did so. I let her go, allowing the bitch ninety seconds to do what she wist. By hap, I caught sight just then of a comely wench in a much-too-short skirt. These things do very often come to my notice somehow. Nor was her face greatly inferior to her legs. I gave her an "eight" on my ten-scale and made a lewd noise for her. Of New York coffee houses, this was far from the worst. The diversity coefficient was getting better, too, and therefore I decided to finish my coffee after all.

In the end, I had to wait more than ninety seconds for my accomplice to return and begin primping with her comb and blushers and eyelash extenders, etc., as if she imagined the place was full of prosperous bachelors. Outside, the snow had begun to come down in a way that was neither especially exaggerated nor the other way around. It was in fact just about perfect for those who go in for that sort of thing. The wind, too, always invisible, could be measured by the effects it produced. How strange all things are! Quantum physics, black holes, me in New York City.

"Let us arise then, you and I, and sally out where the sunrise looks like a patient cauterized upon a table," I admonished, curious to see if she recognized the line I had mangled. I did leave a tip for the waiter but failed to exit the place without paying the bill. I doubt I had consumed more than two bits worth of actual coffee, all the rest owing to overhead, labor, shipping, advertisement, and the sort. My old grandmother used to provide the first cup free of charge.

"Hold it!" said I, once we had returned to the street. "I need to piss."

"Such a charmer you are. No really, I have to get back to work now."

My patience almost at an end, I turned her about and conducted us back to the coffee place so recently abandoned. The clientele had not significantly changed during our half-minute absence, and I was gratified by the welcoming smiles that awaited us. But of course, the men's facility now had a man in it, a ruffled sort of individual with an odious tie. I waited for him, counting the moments till he had peed to completion and had restored himself. He wasn't even wearing underwear, the filth. His bladder must have been larger than a pumpkin. Would I, or would I not be able to return to the street and collect the bitch before too late?

I would not. Turning westward, I hurried forward against the resistance of the crowd, never spying her till almost too late. I was and am old and heavy while she is and was notably spry for a woman of a certain kind.

"Alright!" I hollered, "and just where do you think *you're* going?"

She turned and—believe me—laughed in my face. She was enjoying this. Had she been just ten years older and me ten younger . . .

Naw. In any case, we were further now from the place where the editor lived, and I was tired in body, soul, and head. I had certainly had less sleep than the bitch, and even she was lagging.

"What kind of person are you?" she asked suddenly. "I mean really?"

We proceeded apace, resorting to the underground at 1:52 and driving uptown for fourteen stops. We emerged into a doleful district, doleful even by local standards, and stepped past a series of delicatessens, bodegas, sausage shops, and the like. Here, one could smell the pickles and sauerkraut, the smoked meats and aromatic pies, and for a moment I was threatened with the temptation to invest in some of these materials. I saluted a fat man in an apron, a merry person who smiled back at me wildly.

"Want to stop and get something to eat?" the bitch asked.

"Certainly. But we aren't going to do that."

"Hound. You aren't as much fun as I thought you might be."

"Just keep walking."

We had crossed 127th Street, and I could detect still further intersections up ahead. A few miles further and we'd have been inside the Arctic Circle. God, I hate this town. A quantity of snow had meantime found a way into my left shoe and had set about victimizing my toes. God, I hate this weather. What good is weather when one wants simply to read books, eat pastries, and listen to fine music? It was not terribly late as yet, but already the city's sputtering searchlights had been ignited, setting the snowflakes, as it were, on fire. And, too, there were those immensely tall radio and internet towers spangled with green and lilac lights. You add these to the bookstores and the fundamental wretchedness of New York City might be half-allayed.

And so, in the fullness of time and availing ourselves of a taxicab, we arrived at 237th Street where a number of sights were on display. The soil here, the little bit that I could discover between the cement slabs, was leached and pale, too anemic to support even the most primitive of lichens, much less flowers. I took up a pinch of the stuff and, confessedly, found it more friable than I might have guessed. Still, we proceeded forward, advancing further and further into the colder and colder north, moving slowly among geographical features both east and west. Despite the rather interesting-looking overhead apartments, some with double-glazed windows, this did not at all appear to me the proper address for even a low-rent editor.

"How much further do we have to go?" I asked politely. "Goddamn it!"

"Not much further. Okay, a little bit further. Actually, I think we should go back."

"Just keep walking."

We passed into an unappealing zone, a drear area with advertisements in unprecedented languages. The women wore scarves and would not look a person in the face. An ordinary blimp just then passed overhead trailing a banner promoting a brand of software. Needing to eliminate, I moved into the space between one of the pizza parlors whereupon the bitch thought to use the opportunity to run away. I wasn't prompt enough to catch her, not until a kindly police officer, seeing the issue, hasted to my aid. Came then two, no three noisy ambulances in tandem, their flashing blue lights adding to my delight. I have explained my love of clashing colors.

"How much further?" I asked.

"Just keep walking."

We arrived at length to a collateral street full of an extensive manufacturing plant that continued on for perhaps a hundred yards before then bending sharply at the building's "elbow," to make that comparison. What was being produced here behind those smoked windows remained one of the things we never discovered. Finally, finally, finally, we came to the address corresponding to the notation the bitch had inscribed in the palm of her hand. It was a tilted structure with a combined lightning rod and a weathervane in the shape of a domestic animal. The date of erection, the building's erection, was posted on the door. More elderly than I realized, I climbed with difficulty to the porch where a large stone frog had been set to guard the door. It was not really a sinister-looking artifact, so I looked the thing in the face and then checked my own image in the door's wrinkled glass pane, an antique appliance significantly thicker at bottom than at the top. (Not many people understand that glass is a liquid actually, albeit somewhat a viscous one.) Three times I knocked politely, reasonably politely, before at last using my voice. We did not of course expect anyone actually to come to the door, or anyway not until we had forced the issue. Peering into the dour interior of that one-time business establishment of some kind, I could make out the floor-to-ceiling shelving that must at one time have been used to house things. I also detected a parrot's cage, now devoid of birds, dangling from the ceiling by a silver cord. Did anyone still live here I asked, speaking to myself alone.

"He's gone," the bitch advised. "No one lives here anymore. Useless. We need to get back. It'll be dark in about . . . forty-five minutes."

I examined my own watch, but it was not yet dark enough for the luminescence to have kicked in. Behind me, two ambulances, presumably carrying fresh burdens, were racing back in the direction from which they had likely come. Against the snow-endowed sky, I perceived a half-dozen asterisk-shaped clouds, like gears they seemed, rotating slowly. At that moment, the building contracted and groaned out loud, causing me to jump back a short distance. My esteem for the editor increased; all my life I have wanted to dwell in the strangest possible houses.

"What a dump!" my colleague described. A philistine of the first water, she would have used cuneiform tablets for shotgun practice. For the remainder of the day, I offered her neither cigarette stubs nor any blunts soever. I had meanwhile observed a seam of light spreading across the parlor floor, which was not even to mention an empty beer can positioned on the coffee table. But how could I believe the can was in fact actually empty? Suddenly, I reached out to forestall the bitch from running away again. Because the can was upside down.

If there were really any editors domiciled in this queer structure, this would have been an apposite time for such to reveal themselves. Instead, a full minute went past, the inapposite sun going down an inch an hour. I needed to piss, but the door was locked.

"Don't look," said I to the bitch. "I'm fixing to piss on the door itself."

She did (turn away) but didn't go so far that I couldn't haul her back. As always, I was aware of the world-girdling underground ocean running past at high speed. And that, necessarily, was when the editor opened the door so quickly that I had trouble shutting off the flow.

He was, it proved, an ordinary case of a very odd human being. With his ears and other parts, we both of us jumped back a few inches. Normally, we expect people's noses to be in the usual location.

"Come on in!" he said robustly in that voice of his. "In! In! In! But don't ask about Foib's new novel."

Taking the bitch in my stronger hand, we pushed past the editor and then came to a stop in the proximate center of the parlor. First the books—scads and scads of them in well-burnished covers. I dashed for them but was restrained by the almighty hand of a midget robot appearing from out of nowhere.

"I just wanted to look! Just wanted to look, I say," said I, "at some of those books. Especially that big yellow sucker."

"Later. Much later. But first I need to ask, or anyway want to ask what has inspired you to interfere in these affairs."

"Okay."

"Okay, what?"

"Go ahead and ask."

"Very well, what has inspired you to inquire into such things? Random curiosity? Or more evil intentions?"

"I think *you're* evil, truth be told."

"It's obvious who the evil one is. Hey! Did I say you could sit?"

I leapt up with alacrity. Me evil? I don't think so. It *is* true that I experienced a filthy dream recently, and not my first one either, but that weighs as nothing compared to the books I've read. Had this monster with scales for skin even just once tackled Hodgkin's *History of Italy and her Invaders*?

"Alright, how long before I *can* sit? I'm not as young as . . ."

". . . as you used to be? Christ, Vade, I had expected more originality from you. Not one single person is as young as . . ."

". . . as one used to be?"

"Precisely. Aright, you can sit now. Not you, her. Want a drink? You used to like banana daiquiris."

He went for it, allowing me to go to the bookcase and take down that faint yellow tome that had been nagging at me for the past half-hour. (Later, I learned that this remarkable man some years earlier had engineered a "cut-out," or "capsule," he called it of some fifteen years of the Seventeenth Century and had added it to his own experience.) I unsealed the book, turned the cover, read the title and imprint information, and then scurried back to my place. Another half-minute having gone past, I returned to the bookshelves and read another spate of good-quality prose impressed in a fourteen-point Times New Roman font. I have not remembered the author's name, save that it had a Sanskrit flavor.

The daiquiri, once delivered to me, proved of decent quality and gave off a febrile but autumnal afflatus that went direct to the enjoyment centers of the mind. I took a sizeable gulp and gargled with it. Noticing my happiness, our host also drank, a fluid as yellow as his book.

"The bitch has gone," he said.

"What!"

"The bitch has gone," he said.

"What!"

"While you were fuddling with my yellow book."

I cursed and stood, by no means certain that I would ever be able without guidance to find my way back to headquarters.

"You're not really Streicher" he went on. "Not really. Hell, I can see the rubber band."

"Possibly. But could we not talk about Foib? You published him after all, no?"

"Some of the better stuff. Stuff he wrote while he was drunk. That part was easy to upload."

"Upload. I'm getting nervous."

"Your ice has almost melted. Want another dose of this good liquor? We can't discuss things until we're relaxed. Me, I've been relaxed since I was nine."

"Upload? Talk about that."

"Oh, for goodness sakes. You can't expect a man to write anything after he's dead. Or, did you?"

"You uploaded his thoughts after he was dead. I see. And no doubt transcribed them yourself. Aw, come on man!"

He capsized with laughter.

"Transcribe? No, thank you; we have our escrubilator for that."

The man's wife, if that is what she was, appeared just then in the doorway, remaining too briefly for anyone to describe her. Her negroidal hair was very long and had coalesced, as it were, into a buzzard's nest, to speak so. Let it be reported that her nostrils were of unlike size as also her remarkably protruding nipples. Her dress was of the usual stuff, but her two shoes seemed not to have been designed for feet. She wore neither hats nor gloves nor were her bracelets greatly to wonder at.

"Good evening!" said I. It was almost evening by this time and the sun, reduced by now to a mere red seed of about the size of a collar button, was dropping speedily oceanward. Very far away in terms of distance, I could discern the mushroom-like apartment buildings of Manhattan, Brooklyn, and Staten Island. For one insane moment, I enjoyed believing that I could even see my own sanctuary and, ridiculously, a critical mass of my hallmates. Bringing myself back to reality, I pushed back and finished off my drink.

"In which direction did she actually go?" I asked. "The bitch I mean?"

"A couple grams of coke and daiquiris taste even better."

"No, no, thanks all the same. Much obliged. It doesn't mix real well with serotonin, don't you know."

"Dopamine perhaps?"

Why was the varlet so accommodating? My suspicions put on new growth.

"Christ! He's just trying to be hospitable!" his woman said. "You feel me?"

I said nothing, not until I said, "Where's that second drink we were just mentioning?"

We sat and drank and talked about literature. Just because the parrot cage was empty, it didn't mean it didn't once have something in it. My host was still talking when his wife on two occasions moved out of the frame of the discussion, never coming back again. I watched admiringly as she set about climbing the steep staircase piled with books.

"Fine woman, your wife."

"Mother, actually. Now, if you were really Streicher, you'd have had more than just one drink by now. Why not just take off that mask and let us have a look at you?"

"'Us'?"

"You and me."

"I already know what *I* look like! What I don't know is how *you* look!"

"Just as you see me."

"Oh? You say so? You think I don't see that rubber band?"

He looked down. Behind the mask, we may presume he was blushing.

"Alright," I allowed finally. "Let me see yours, and you can see mine. You can't ask for better than that."

He thought about it. "And my mother?"

"Yes, yes, bring her on down, and let us look at her, too."

She did come, climbing slowly down the bookcluttered staircase. From my point of view, I could detect her advanced age and some of the little scars denoting the facial surgeries she had endured. To this day, I do not know the title of any of those books. They were too far away.

"Get your ass on down here!" I suggested. "I'm fixing to expose my real face."

We drew near, one of us to each other, the editor and me. My mask had been exacerbating me for some

while, and I anticipated that I'd be pleased to be free of
it. But which of the two geniuses would be first to reveal himself to each other?

In the event, I took another swig of molten ice. The
cubes themselves, in desperate condition, crashed into
my nose. Meantime Shostakovich, or a recording rather, was playing in the enormous background of this
real-life scene that bent to one side. I espied the crim-
son bust of Pallas over the chamber door. Save for her,
there was but one other woman in the home, not mentioning we two men. I wasn't unduly alarmed; my revolver was in easy reach, and I remained confident in
the strength I used to have in my fists. We drew yet
nearer, leaving less than contagion distance between
we twain. My own distance had been considerable at
one time, but we were not here for that purpose.

The music came finally to a crescendo, inciting us to
rip off our masks all at once.

"Gorblimey!" we said, each now viewing the other's
true nature at last. Never ashamed of my own good
looks, pretty good, I allowed it to be seen from both
sides. But it was the publisher's face that filled my
drawers with piss. Some years previous, ago, I had seen
the face of a common housefly under high magnifica-
tion.

"So, this," I retorted humorously, "is what genius
looks like."

The mother-fucker (speaking truthfully), blushed
and laughed.

We dined that night on pickled hinny and a good
salad compiled of avocado, oyster parts, ripe olives, and
artichoke hearts. The oil was good, too, and highly
reminiscent of Greece and/or Italy. But all this was as
nothing when compared to the dessert, a freight of
pink and green *petit fours* with syrup cores. Afflicted

with an unmeasurable liking for sweet things, I must have absorbed half a dozen of them before they were subtracted from the table. Now, now finally, the editor took up a cigar and ignited it. Seldom have I whiffed an odor as odious as that one.

"We need to talk now," he said, pushing back his chair and lounging in it in a more or less obscene fashion. Jewish beyond all doubt, he had three blue warts athwart his unstinted nose. "Talk about *serious matters.*"

I asked for another drink. The music had reverted to "The Tennessee Waltz," and I was myself feeling more mellow than since two or three hours ago. The rectum had meantime poured me two drams of cognac, some of which I conserved in that cavity where one of my fillings had fallen out.

"Serious matters," he went on. "Old Thucydides, for example, died long before he finished his history. How do you think that happened? Hm?"

"He did *not*, that man, finish his history! Xenophon did that."

"He finished a great deal, however. And finished it after he died. Or after he died in the popular sense."

I wanted to kick his shin and would have done so had I been just a few months younger. The malefactor continued to talk:

"No, he had not got past the death of Antiphobus when he collapsed. No, it was *us*, always us, who took up the task. Not that we get any great appreciation for it."

"Fascinating. And now, I think I'd like to trudge off to bed about now. Tired. And my feet are sore. You know how that is. Tired?"

"These men, these Thucydides and the sort, they were just corpses when we took over. Corpses. Like you."

I glared. His glare was more powerful than mine, as I am bounden to admit. I finished off my ice and tried to use the voided glass as a telescope, to speak so. Even then, I couldn't overbear the force of his vermillion eyes.

"Who *are* you?" I respectfully inquired. "No, I mean really?"

"And Wagner. You don't imagine he did *Parsifal*, do you, before syphilis ruint his head?"

I had drunk too much, and it was easy for him to push me down again. The ceiling, as I now saw for the first time, had faces painted on it, demons mostly.

"And you," he pursued, "you have some accomplishments of your own, *nicht wahr?*"

"Me? Hardly. I can't read Russian any better than English."

"The books. You're read a lot of books I'm told. A very great many of books. Thick ones."

The wife/mother had come back again; I could see her lurking at the top of the stairs.

"She's back," I said.

"And in several languages."

"Greek, you mean? And Chinese? Lots of people do that."

"And your translation of the *Suda?*"

"Partial translation. It were of course the original authors. The better ones, who deserve the acclaim."

"Too modest!"

"Never been accused of that!"

I asked for and was given a yellow cigar. I wasn't opposed to these things, provided they didn't conflict with my prescriptions. Night was not so far away that I could safely ignore my sleeping arrangements. Meantime, I continued to confuse the moon and sun, the pane was that thick.

"Too modest. All those books. We need that."

"Possibly. But I never actually *created* anything. Nothing!"

"But just think what others might create with your wide learning. We did it with Herodotus."

"I'm getting nervous again."

"Not at all! There's no pain Vade. And your achievement will endure forever, for as long as cloud computing remains in effect.

"Are you trying to tell me . . . ?"

"The supreme compliment Mr. Mecum. And no pain. Or very little anyway."

"But . . . But . . . "

"Qubits. Parallel qubits in fuzzy permutation."

"Great Scott! But they're so small, qubits are."

"So are kidney stones."

"O, Lord. Look, I need to go home and think about this for a certain time."

He laughed out loud. The mother had taken up by the door where she stood standing with folded arms.

"But what about my friends?"

"Taw, we could use him. The others, no."

"Good Lord! But I'm only 78 years old!"

"Yes, and look at you. A skein of guts with a rotting memory. Hell man, you can't even get it up anymore!"

"Look, there's something you need to understand!"

"What?"

"Anything! Okay, I want to see my lawyer."

"Oh, for goodness sakes, do try to calm down. We won't be taking immediate action. No, we intend to give you enough time to set down in your own words what you've been thinking all these years right up until this time. How's your penmanship?"

"Lord, Lord, Lord. Never thought it would come to this."

"No pain. Or very little anyway. And don't worry about your dog."

"That is not, and I repeat *not* my dog!"

"We can send him over with you, if you want. Or is it a 'she'?"

"Jesus Christ shit son-of-a bitch! What sort of people are you after all?"

"Patient people, that's what we are. And I suggest you take advantage of that. Here now, take these pages and two ballpoint pens and follow Mac into the next room. There's an oaken desk and waste basket in there, and a standard bed with a foam rubber pillow. Take two hours and tell us everything you've thought and done these past many years. Or everything you've thought anyway."

Ten

I passed through the kitchen, retrieving two pink *petits fours* on the way. Mac followed close behind, an object in her hand. There *was* a bed, a waste basket, and a bust of Empedocles on the desk. The pillow was as described.

"Well," said I, "think I'll just sit here and write out an account of my thinking over the mentioned period. But first, I need to piss."

She pointed me to a kidney-shaped urn in the corner. Never able to piss when a member of her gender is watching, I faked the process and returned to the desk. It did not by any means seemed oaken to me. Bringing my drink with me, I sat and began right away to scribble: "I don't really have anything to say to those who house their books in *metal* shelving."

I worked diligently until about eleven and then asked to go outside. The landscape is startling in these upper reaches of the city, and I wanted to set it down in memory as a safeguard against ever coming back again. Here again, as in other places, either a moth had gotten trapped in the doorknob, or something was askew inside my head. Returning to my apportioned desk, I wrote it down as simply an affect of genius, or too much reading perpetuated over far too long a time.

ABOUT THE AUTHOR

Tito Perdue was born in 1938 in Chile, the son of an electrical engineer from Alabama. The family returned to Alabama in 1941, where Tito graduated from the Indian Springs School, a private academy near Birmingham, in 1956. He then attended Antioch College in Ohio for a year, before being expelled for cohabitating with a female student, Judy Clark. In 1957, they were married, and remain so today. He graduated from the University of Texas in 1961, and spent some time working in New York City, an experience which garnered him his life-long hatred of urban life. After holding positions at various university libraries, Tito has devoted himself full-time to writing since 1983.

His first novel, 1991's *Lee*, received favorable reviews in *The New York Times*, *The Los Angeles Reader*, and *The New England Review of Books*. In addition to the present volume, his novels include *The New Austerities* (1994), *Opportunities in Alabama Agriculture* (1994), *The Sweet-Scented Manuscript* (2004), *Fields of Asphodel* (2007), *The Node* (2011), *Morning Crafts* (2013), *Reuben* (2014), the *William's House* quartet (2016), *Cynosura* (2017), *Philip* (2017), *Though We Be Dead, Yet Our Day Will Come* (2018), *The Bent Pyramid* (2018), *The Philatelist* (2018), *The Smut Book* (2018), *The Gizmo* (2019), *Love Song of the Australopiths* (2020), and *Journey to a Location* (2021)—which have been praised in *Chronicles: A Magazine of American Culture*, *The Quarterly Review*, *The Occidental Observer*, and at *Counter-Currents*.

In 2015, he received the H. P. Lovecraft Prize for Literature.

www.ingramcontent.com/pod-product-compliance
Lightning Source LLC
Chambersburg PA
CBHW021931170626
46807CB00007B/3066